Primordial Soup Kitchen

A Collection of Short Strangeness

By Todd Downing

FIRST EDITION

ISBN: 978-0-9981989-9-6

Edited by Raechelle Downing & Andrea Edelman

Cover design by Todd Downing
(Original photo credit DarkworkX)

WWW.TODDDOWNING.COM

Deep7 Press is a subsidiary of Despot Media, LLC
1214 Woods Rd SE Port Orchard, WA 98366 USA
WWW.DEEP7.COM

*For my fellow lovers of
the strange and unusual,
the random and profane*

CONTENTS

Should We Pass This Way Again

જી

She reached forward, extending a slender, motorized, chrome-covered hand in a graceful mechanical motion. She pressed the button on the glove compartment, and the small hatch lowered slowly on hydraulic arms, revealing its contents: a hundred digital data cards, neatly aligned and organized according to type.

"Look," said the man, pointing a shiny metal finger out her window, gesturing at the sprawling industrial complex with its billowing smokestacks and towering spires. He lifted a metal foot from the accelerator, reaching up mechanically with a reflective chrome hand to scratch an imagined itch on his gleaming steel forehead as the vehicle slowed. "Don't we remember that place?" he asked, his voice module hollow and electronic. "Before the complex, I mean."

"I think so," she said. "I was about to pop one in myself. Would you like to join me?"

"Yes," he replied.

She selected two of the small, square memory cards that had been labeled identically, drawing them out as the glove compartment door whirred shut. She pulled down the passenger-side sun visor, peering at her reflection in the tiny vanity mirror. The silver gleam of metal and two glowing crimson LEDs stared back at her, and she flipped the side panel on her head to the open position.

He did the same, and together they inserted the cards.

"I remember now," he said.

"So do I. What do you remember?"

He turned his head and watched the suddenly empty field as it sped by. "I remember baseball," he said.

"So do I. And tag."

"Yes," he recalled, the card reader whirring in his head. "Tag."

"Do you remember when we first made love on the hill?" she asked. "With the stars bright and the wind cool on our backs?"

"I remember," he replied. "And the time it rained and we had to run naked to the car?"

"Oh yes," she chuckled, and the sound was from a sitcom laugh track. "I remember."

"I have some good memories of this place," he said quietly, almost eluding her audio sensors.

"Yes, so do I," she replied. "I remember coming here with our children, and playing touch football and flying kites. And you used to throw a tennis ball for the dog."

He nodded a semblance of agreement. "Yes. Our dog, Jake. And we would bring a picnic, with tuna sandwiches and deviled eggs and coleslaw. And we would take short day hikes out to the river."

She turned her chrome head to face him, and their glowing red LEDs met, brightening in unison. "I miss those days," she said, turning back toward the window as he shifted into gear.

"So do I," he admitted. "It was nice of the company to include those with our purchase."

"Yes, it was."

And then they were still, and silent, and the car hummed along the highway.

There was a soft click, followed by another, and he popped his card out and handed it to her. She replaced the memories carefully in the glove compartment, and flipped the visor back up to the ceiling. She leaned over on the door, resting her shiny, chrome chin in a metallic palm.

The reflection of her glowing eyes in the passenger window caught his attention, and he reached out to touch the cold steel of her neck. "Are you alright?"

Her reply was slow and melancholy. "Yes. I like those memories."

"So do I. We'll use them, should we pass this way again."

She nodded, and he returned his attention to the road. They were silent again for a time, and then she stirred once more. "Sometimes," she sighed, "I can almost remember without them."

"Sometimes," he affirmed, servos whining as he rested his steel hand on the round crest of the steering wheel, "I can too."

∞

Written in 1990, originally published in *Midnight Zoo* literary magazine in 1992. A conceptual short-short inspired by early computer animation and '80s techno music, this piece still makes me smile.

Edward Biddle Takes on the World

ℭ

Not another nightmare.

Please, not another one.

Not another REM-induced scenario of guilt and terror, with an all-star cast of people I don't know, have never met and haven't a single ounce of regard for. No more vicious, bloodthirsty housewives wielding glistening steak knives in their wobbly, fattened arms, screaming so loud my head bursts open as they thrust the shiny bit of steel at my chest.

Screaming all the while, "You deserve it! You deserve it!"

All I want is for the screaming to end.

STOP the screaming.

Edward Biddle rolled over in bed, drawing the sheets with him in his tightly clenched fists, leaving his wife exposed to the cold morning air. She stirred and reluctantly blinked her eyes open. Twisting her head toward the nightstand, she noted the red digital numbers on the clock radio: 6:30 a.m.

Right on schedule.

She smiled and swung her feet tiredly to the floor. She didn't know what it was that occupied her husband's dreams, that made him roll over and steal the covers each morning precisely at 6:30, but it was certainly less jarring than the electronic siren or blast of loud rock music from the clock radio, and she hoped it would continue as it had for the past five years.

Reaching delicately toward the foot of the bed, she gently pulled her satin robe around her pale, slender shoulders and rose to greet the day, shutting the bedroom door silently as she left Edward to rise on his own.

Edward's eyes were a blur of motion beneath closed lids. Why? Why was it happening to him? These were not his dreams. These were not his fantasies. None of these women were his wife.

This was not his problem.

He snapped his eyes open, forcing himself awake. It was the only way to avoid the nightmares anymore. Since his thirtieth birthday, exactly five years ago today, the dreams had gotten worse, become more frequent and horrible. He found that after a while, no sleep at all was better than eight hours of this mindless torture. Why him? He'd had a normal, idyllic childhood, never had so much as a drag from a cigarette or a drop of alcohol—but wasn't uptight about it either. He was in top physical condition, ran two miles a day and played racquetball on the weekends. He was financially secure in a job that he liked. He owned a two-bedroom house in the suburbs, his car was paid for and his wife adored him (he thought). Why, then, was a simple night's sleep so hard to come by?

Edward blinked, and the swirling fog of slumber continued to dance before his eyes—or was it the steam from his wife's shower? He yawned, hoisting his body into a sitting position on the edge of the bed and stretching his bare arms out toward his knees.

Christ, it's cold.

He stood, knees popping as he brought his weight forward, blue jockey shorts hanging loosely around his hips.

What the sweet Christ is all this mist?

He waved his hand, fanning the fog in front of him, suddenly realizing he could no longer see the bedroom wall. Or the bed. Or the door.

The distant cry of a tropical bird rang out of the mist, somewhere to his left, and Edward Biddle knew he was not in Kansas anymore. Or anywhere in the United States, for that matter. He frowned, inhaling lungs full of stinging air, and he could smell the heady fumes of diesel fuel and burning plastic.

What the hell...?

Then the fog became orange smoke, and Edward heard the steady cadence of a helicopter's spinning rotor blade. The alien breeze whipped the hair on his head and gradually the wafting signal smoke cleared to reveal a dense jungle countryside, littered with the bloody, twisted bodies of dead men clad in broken helmets and shredded olive drab uniforms. He raised his head and saw the hovering chopper, and the ear-shattering pop of gunfire erupted from the trees.

Now hold on a second...

The battle cry of a hundred ARVN soldiers rang out, and Edward Biddle felt panic rise in his throat. His stomach churned and spasmed with fear, and as he watched, the helicopter exploded in a million hurling pyrotechnic fragments, flaming bits of metal and flesh whizzing past him.

He turned away from the blast, and the soldiers charged.

This can't be! he thought, his breath coming in quick gulps. I'm in Vietnam. In my underwear.

This can NOT be!

The loud report of blazing rifles filled the air, and Edward's eyes welled up with heavy tears. He fell to his knees, clutching his face and weeping angrily.

"*No!* It's a mistake! I wasn't in Vietnam! This is someone else's nightmare! *This is someone else's flashback!!*"

And suddenly he was back in his room, and he could feel the twisted, knotted sheets between his knees. He could see the open bedroom door, hear the sizzle of bacon frying in the kitchen, smell its wonderful enticing odor.

"Honey?" his wife called. "Breakfast..."

Edward Biddle drew a large breath, and gradually felt his sweat discontinue and the movement in his stomach subside. Well! he thought. THAT was interesting... He carefully slid from the bed and went to the open closet to pull out his clothes for the day.

The kitchen was silent and still, and Edward's wife pulled up a chair across the table from him. "What were you dreaming about?"

"Oh, you know," Edward answered, calmly pressing his tie flat against his shirtfront as he gingerly sipped his coffee. "The usual." He wasn't wild about the idea of his wife knowing the full impact of his nightmares, and was genuinely afraid of upsetting her. He sincerely hoped that the problem, like a school bully, would go away if he ignored it long enough. "How about that bacon," he smiled.

His wife shot him a confused glance. He raised his eyes to meet hers, and she giggled at his sober expression. "I thought you were serious there for a moment," she laughed.

Edward frowned. "I am serious. I smelled you cooking bacon this morning. Where is it?"

"That's not funny, dear," she scolded, visibly shaken by his grim attitude. "You know you can't have bacon. The doctor said that since you're at risk for another heart attack, we have to cut down on your fat intake."

Edward swallowed hard, choking on his coffee. "What do you mean, another heart attack? I've never had a heart attack. I'm in perfect health."

His wife furrowed her brow in a sad look of perplexity and worry. "Oh, dear. The doctor said you might go through a denial stage."

"Denial," Edward spat, "I'm not denying anything! I'm just saying I was looking forward to some bacon with my breakfast! Jesus! What's wrong with the world?!"

"Well," she said softly, "denial or not, I won't be an accessory to your killing yourself. We haven't had bacon in this house for two years and I'm not about to start getting it. Now hurry, or you'll miss your train."

Edward rolled his eyes. All right, what's going on? Am I still dreaming, or what?

"Honey," he explained tiredly, "I don't take the train. I drive to work."

She shook her head, chuckling sadly. "In what car?"

Edward sighed in frustration. He'd had quite enough of this nonsense. "In the car that is parked in the driveway outside," he boomed. "The car I just paid off last month! *Our car!*"

He rose, toppling the chair and throwing his napkin on the table in disgust. He didn't stop to kiss her, didn't say goodbye, just turned and dashed out the front door, swinging his briefcase behind him. "See?" he pointed, more to himself than his wife whom he'd left inside. The car was in the driveway, precisely where he'd left it, complete with the oil spot on the concrete underneath. He went to the trunk, fishing his keys from his left pants pocket. "Crazy woman," he mumbled as he inserted the key and the trunk clicked open. He grasped the lip with his left hand and hauled it upward, swinging the heavy briefcase toward the vacant cargo space with his right.

Suddenly Edward tensed, and his eyes grew wide. The briefcase halted in mid-air, and his jaw dropped in horror. The body of a middle-aged man lay bound and gagged, crammed like a rag doll just below the spare tire, deathly pale, open eyes red and bloodshot.

There was a bullet wound in his forehead.

Edward gasped, let out a frightened whimper, then gasped again. His breathing accelerated, and his legs began to feel wobbly. Then he heard the far-off wail of a police siren, and he slammed the trunk down, dropping the briefcase to the pavement.

What the hell is going on—?!

His vision blurred slightly, and he lost his balance, falling down hard against the car. Before he could regain his bearings, the patrol vehicles were screeching up to the curb, and every cop in the city was leaping onto the sidewalk, guns and clubs pointed in Edward's direction.

He tried to stand, and was thrown against the car again, his hands wrenched up behind his head. He could feel the hard slaps against his ribs and legs as a sheriff's deputy patted him down.

"What have we here, Mr. Palmer?" smiled the deputy as he reached inside Edward's jacket, producing a small .45 pistol from the breast pocket.

"I'm not Mr. Palmer," Edward tried to explain, but his voice was weary and confused. "That's not my gun..."

And then his hands were cuffed tightly behind him, and he heard the monotonous drone of another officer reciting his rights.

"Look," he pleaded, gesturing vaguely with his shoulders, "check my ID. In my right rear pocket."

The deputy smiled, and his response was right out of Edward's last nightmare. "I already checked, buddy. You weren't carrying any ID."

Oh no! he thought as the deputy opened the door of the squad car and pushed Edward into it. *I left my wallet on the dresser!*

He watched dazedly from the backseat of the patrol car as the police swarmed over his automobile, snapping photos of the dead body in the trunk.

And the sheriff said, "Groovy. We've got his prints on the weapon. Get homicide down here."

Those aren't my fingerprints, he thought. *I don't even own a gun.*

He heard the roar of an engine, and suddenly he was being whisked away down silent city streets, listening helplessly as the two officers in front offered their short-sighted opinions on the case.

"He looks guilty to me," said one.

"Well we caught him with the murder weapon and the body in his trunk," offered the other.

"Think he'll fry?"

"Dunno. Depends on his defense. Kingpins like Palmer back there can buy some pretty convincing testimony."

"Excuse me," Edward chimed, scooting forward to address the two policemen through the metal screen. "I think there's been a big mistake here. My name isn't Palmer. It's Biddle. Edward Biddle. I'm an accountant."

The first officer laughed and the second one said something about saving it for the judge.

The ride was short and unpleasant, mostly because Edward's nose itched and he could do nothing to alleviate the torturous affliction. Just as he figured out how to tuck his plagued proboscis into the crook of his shoulder and let the car's vibration do the work for him, the vehicle came to a halt in front of the downtown police station and the officers dragged him from the back seat.

Before he knew it, he was on his feet, stumbling across the sidewalk and through the front doors, up a flight of stairs and into the sergeant's office. Then he was in a straight wooden chair, his hands unbound, staring up at a corpulent police sergeant as the large, porcine man wolfed down a salami sandwich and a cup of coffee. The sergeant leaned an enormous buttock on the edge of his desk, and Edward could hear it creak and groan pitifully under the stress.

"Listen, Drake," he mumbled through shreds of Wonder Bread and greasy bits of salami, drooling slightly from the right corner of his mouth. "I don't want to keep you here any more than you want to be here. Just tell me where the statue is hidden, and I'll let you go, acceptable?"

Edward shook his head in resignation. "My name is Edward Biddle. I'm an accountant."

The sergeant laughed, spewing small chunks of his wet mouthful into the air. "Yeah, right. And my name is Elmer J. Fudd, millionaire. I own a mansion and a yacht."

Edward sighed, and another tear gathered in his eye. "It's all a big mistake."

The sergeant swallowed, leaning forward with his fat, sweaty hands resting on a pair of bloated knees. "Look. Drake. You've been a good cop, aside from this one little infraction. And I know you've been under a lot of stress lately. I think you ought to go see the station psychiatrist. I'm sure she can help you out."

"My name," Edward repeated, "is Biddle. I'm not a cop, I'm an accountant. And I don't know anything about a missing statue."

The sergeant rose, beckoning Edward to his feet. The man's look was one of sympathy, and Edward felt he could be trusted.

"I don't know anything about a dead body or a gun or a heart attack or anything..." he pleaded. "You've gotta believe me."

"Hey, I believe you, buddy," the Sergeant affirmed, resting a wide hand on Edward's weak and sagging shoulder. "Let's just take a walk down the hall."

Edward nodded in compliance, and the two ambled slowly out of the bustling office and down a narrow corridor, stopping in front of a door marked DR. STEVENSON.

The sergeant knocked sharply a couple of times, and a woman's voice answered back.

"Come in."

Edward looked uncertainly at the large man, and the sergeant smiled back at him. "Go on, buddy. She'll help you."

Edward Biddle opened the door and entered a dimly lit office with blinds and a ceiling fan. A commodious leather couch sat near one wall, and a slender brunette woman sat officially behind a great desk, scribbling notes on a yellow legal pad. She looked up, smiled and beckoned him to the couch, and Edward closed the door softly behind him.

He sat down slowly, feeling his legs creak as he did so. "I'm glad to talk to somebody who can help," he said nervously.

"Well, I'm glad to be of assistance," she affirmed. "Now, I've been reviewing your defense, and I think we can plea bargain a life sentence instead of the chair."

Edward gasped and his eyes widened again. "WHAT?!"

"Don't tell me you want to fry," she said, cocking her head in bewilderment.

Edward suddenly felt very sick again. "No, I don't want to fry, I haven't done anything! You're supposed to be a psychiatrist—"

"I beg your pardon?" she snapped. "I am your defense attorney, Mr. Palmer, and you don't have to do the insanity act with me."

"Get me a doctor," Edward protested. "I want to see a doctor."

"What the hell are you talking about—"

Edward leapt to his feet, waving his arms wildly in the air. "NOW!" he bellowed, spittle flying from his mouth in tiny drops. "Get me a doctor NOW!"

The woman stood and backed away toward the office door, a frightened look of consternation in her eyes. "Alright," she answered calmly. "I'll get you a doctor. Just relax, have a seat, and I'll be right back."

Then she was gone, and Edward was tempted to leave as well—just run and get the hell away from there. But where could he go? There were hundreds of cops outside, and every one of them thought he was a hit man named Palmer. Except the sergeant, who thought he was some bad cop called Drake.

He decided to relax and take his chances with the doctor.

Within seconds, the woman returned, followed closely by a elderly man in a white lab coat. He looked like something out of a 1960s medical drama, with his black medical bag, stethoscope around his neck. "I'm Dr. Crawford. Your mother here tells me you fell and twisted your ankle at the playground."

Edward rolled his eyes. "Jesus, what is the matter with you people?"

"Roll up your pant leg," the doctor instructed, "let's have a look."

"I'm not rolling up my pant leg, and I'm not playing along with this anymore!"

The doctor smiled a reassuring pediatric smile, and nodded his head. "Fine, that's just fine. You won't play along with this anymore. But if you don't let me take a look at that ankle, you could do a lot more damage to it." As he reached for Edward's pant leg, the doctor turned his head to look at the woman. "Heck of an imagination, Myra. Too bad he's...you know...mentally-challenged."

All right, that's it.

Edward snapped his leg out, slamming the ball of his foot into the doctor's nose, leaving the old man unconscious on the floor. The woman screamed, throwing her hands over a shocked and horrified expression. "Bailey! What have you done?! You naughty, naughty boy!!"

Edward shot up from his seat, grabbing the woman by her shoulders, shaking her firmly. "I am NOT a naughty boy, and I am NOT mentally-challenged! I am NOT a murderer or a cop, and I haven't had a heart attack! I AM, however, one hell of a pissed-off accountant!"

Suddenly the office door burst open, and Edward's wife stormed into the room. "I KNEW I'd find you here. With *her!*" She strode purposefully toward them, stopping just inches from Edward's face.

"Honey," he gaped, almost relieved to see her.

"Don't honey me, you philandering bastard!" she cursed, striking Edward brutally across the cheek with a rather heavy handbag.

He flinched at the pain, and he could feel warm blood as it began to trickle from his nose. "Baby," he pleaded. "Listen to me—"

"No, you listen to me. You want your little painted harlot, you keep her. But don't bother to come home tonight." Turning abruptly on her heel, she marched from the office, slamming the door sharply behind her.

Edward was hot on her trail, flinging open the office door and dashing into the crowded hallway. "Honey?" he squeaked as a mob of reporters pinned him to the wall, shoving cameras and microphones in his face. Bulbs flashed, and Edward found himself temporarily blinded as the voices struck out at him.

"Senator Burton, do you think this is going to hurt your chances of re-election?"

"Look," Edward moaned, "I'm not Senator Burton! You have the wrong guy! This is not my office! This is not my problem! This is not my life!"

But still the questions—someone else's questions—hammered him mercilessly and just as his vision had cleared, another flash exploded in his eyes and suddenly the hallway was quiet.

"Hey, Biddle, you okay?"

Edward rubbed his eyes, trying desperately to clear the big purple tracer from his sight. He slowly turned to face a short, balding man in a suit and tie.

It was Brady, from the advertising department.

Hold on, Edward thought. *I know him! I actually know him!* "Did...did you call me *Biddle?*" he asked.

Brady smiled his broad, toothsome smile and clapped a hand on Edward's shoulder.

"What do ya want me to call you? Sweetheart?" He reached up and thumbed a bit of blood from Edward's upper lip. "Maybe I should call you a cab, huh? You look terrible, Eddy."

Edward grasped Brady by the arms, grinning from ear to ear. "You called me Eddy!"

The short ad man frowned with uncertainty, cocking his head back to take in Edward completely. "That's your name, isn't it?"

"It is!" Edward laughed, almost in tears. "I'm Edward Biddle!"

Brady shook his head. "Look, Biddle. Why don't you take the rest of the day off. I'll cover for you at the meeting. Catch a cab. I'll pick ya up tomorrow morning, okay?"

Edward reached out and hugged Brady close. "I love you, Brady!"

The short executive wriggled free and straightened his tie. "Back at ya, buddy."

Edward Biddle left the office, and he hailed a cab, and he sang out with joy because the driver knew his name. He rode home with a particularly warm sensation of relief in his stomach, gave the driver a twenty from his suit jacket, and told him to keep the change.

As he trod slowly toward the front door, making sure to read the street numbers twice, he sighed and his mood sank.

Would his wife know him?

Would life become normal again?

Were the nightmares and the flashbacks, the mistaken identities finally over?

There was truly only one way to find out.

The door creaked open, and he stepped inside. He could hear the stereo blasting from the living room, and the sound of his wife's vacuuming. He took another step, and another, and he heard the vacuum switch off, coming to a slow, growling halt.

"Honey?" he called tentatively from the entry hall.

"I'm in the living room, dear. How was your day?"

The corners of his mouth turned up slightly and he took a deep breath.

And he wondered who he'd be tomorrow.

ℰↄ

Written in 1990, originally published by Editio Books in 1995. The publisher's acceptance letter called it "an amalgam of *The Twilight Zone* and *Walter Mitty*." As it was written in my twenties, I sometimes look back on it with a cringe, but there's value in showing an evolution in one's work, and so...

Estranged

ℰℭ

Bradley sat, slumped on a couch in a typical suburban living room. A heavyset man in his 40s, a light dusting of gray had begun to invade his copper beard and receding hairline. Flickering, inconstant light from the television played across his haggard features, bags evident under his bespectacled eyes. An untied robe barely covered a disheveled t-shirt, several days unwashed, and baggy sweatpants. His red-rimmed eyes glazed over as Hooper, Quint and Police Chief Brody dealt with a ravenous shark on the screen.

Tina slid onto the sofa beside him without a sound. The ginger twentysomething was slim, hair pulled back in a messy ponytail. Her uniform was pajama pants and a *Rick & Morty* softball tee.

Insomnia was a recent phenomenon for her dad, but she tried to keep her worry hidden.

"Can't sleep?" she asked.

Bradly blinked, but didn't turn from the television. "Hmm? No," he answered.

"What is it this time?"

There was a long beat, and finally Bradley let out a sigh. "I don't... I don't want to go into it."

Tina's brow furrowed. "This is the fourth night in a row."

"I'm aware of that."

His tone was clipped, and she decided to relax the investigation. She regarded the TV screen for a few moments before offering her expert opinion on the situation. "They're gonna need a bigger boat."

Disarmed, Bradly allowed himself a chuckle, showing Tina the father she knew and loved.

"Yeah," he smiled. "That's a lot of fake shark."

Building on her small victory, Tina scooted closer to her dad on the sofa. She leaned over and rested her head on his shoulder. "So what I would do is take a SCUBA tank, and get the shark to take it with its mouth, and I'd shoot it with the rifle, and make it blow up."

"Spoilers," Bradley complained.

Tina pressed on. "And I'd probably say something like, '*Hasta la vista*, baby.'"

Bradley side-eyed his daughter. "Seriously?"

"'I'll be back.'"

"Have you learned nothing?"

"'I am the law.'"

Bradley shook his head. "'You're killing me, Smalls.'"

"Kidding," Tina chuckled. "I know the line."

Bradley nodded, shifting his weight. "Good. I thought I'd failed in my duties."

Tina looked at her father, trying to glean his thoughts from the blank expression on his weary face. Finally, she realized: "You really want me to say it, don't you?"

Bradley stared at the screen. "Hmm?"

"You really need me to say it."

"What?" Bradley turned, his attention finally on his daughter.

Tina nodded at him. "To *you*. You need me to say it to *you*."

"What are you talking about?"

She met his eyes. "Smile, you son of a bitch."

Bradley's face lit up, struck by a bittersweet memory. His mouth revealed a broad smile, which became abject sorrow within moments. He lapsed into sobs, leaning his face into cupped hands.

Tina laid a gentle hand on his quivering shoulder. "Hey," she soothed, "tell me."

"I really miss your mom."

"How long has it been?"

Bradley sniffed, clearing swollen nasal passages. "Couple months. I lost track after a few days."

"I'm sorry, Pop." Tina stroked his arm.

Bradley leaned his head on her shoulder and continued to weep himself to exhaustion.

❧

Tina leaned on the bar of a condo kitchen, watching Eileen prepare a light lunch. A redhead like Tina, Eileen was in her mid-40s, dressed in stylish but unkempt clothing. She seemed to tell the world that she was really trying to care, but wasn't quite there yet.

"I saw Dad," Tina blurted out suddenly.

Eileen froze as if punched in the gut, the air leaving the room like a decompression chamber. Finally, she took a breath, and returned to chopping the celery for her tuna salad. "I don't know why you even go there," she scolded, not looking up from her work.

Tina frowned. "Why would you wonder that? He's my dad."

Eileen put down the knife and found her daughter's eyes. "It's just... Why put yourself through it?"

"Because we're a family and we love each other."

"Family?" Eileen almost spat the word. "Not anymore."

Once again, Tina found herself the go-between, the moderator, the family counselor. "What exactly is the issue here?"

Eileen grabbed a handful of chopped celery and dropped it into the bowl of canned tuna and mayonnaise. "Look," she said flatly, "I really don't need to talk about this right now."

Tina folded her arms defiantly. "I think you really do."

Eileen pounded a delicate fist on the counter, which almost scared her daughter. "It's *over,* Tina. It's done."

"You can't mean that."

"What's done is done," Eileen affirmed. "There's no going back."

Tina hung her head, almost pouting. "I'm sorry, but I don't believe that."

"Well that's just the way it is. Believe what you want."

"I believe we were a family once," Tina challenged, leveling a solemn glare at her mother.

Eileen sighed, tiring of the fight. "And we *were*. But your father checked out. It was his doing, not mine."

"You can't mean that."

"I do."

"Mother."

Eileen returned her daughter's gaze, and it was a look of sadness and surrender. "I do."

Tina frowned, shifting on the bar stool. There was a long pause, and Eileen returned to her tuna salad. Tina watched her for several moments.

Finally, "I asked him to come over."

Eileen's head snapped up in shock, her eyes raging. "You didn't."

Tina returned the look, ounce for ounce, emotion for emotion. "I want you to talk to him."

"How dare you?" Eileen demanded, furious.

"Mother. *Talk to him.*"

Eileen shook her head. "Unbelievable."

"Please," Tina urged. "Just this once. Then I'll drop it."

Eileen paused, letting the silence drive home her daughter's words. Her hands finally shot up in acquiescence. This was clearly happening, and there would be no peace until it did.

"Honey," she said ominously, "this isn't good for anyone. But I'll do it for you."

∞

The small dining room was set for dinner. Tina sat at the head of the table, the ceremonial mediator. Eileen and Bradley, dressed casually, sat across from one another. Eileen did her best to avoid looking at her husband, but he leaned forward, earnest.

"Thank you for inviting me," he said softly.

Tina's eyes roamed from her father to the opposite side of the table. "Mother? He just thanked you."

Eileen stammered, avoiding all eye contact. "I... You're welcome." She shot Tina a look heavy with pathos. "Tina, honey, is this really necessary?"

"Mom, you agreed."

Bradley squirmed uncomfortably. "I'm very sorry, Eileen. Perhaps I should go."

"You stay put, Dad." Tina clasped a hand on his own. "Mom, I'm quite serious about this. You need to open up."

Eileen shook her head in distaste. "But setting an extra place?"

"What are you talking about?" Tina puzzled.

"It's a little morbid..."

"It's for you and Dad to actually have a conversation—"

"Tina," Eileen interrupted, locking eyes with her daughter. "Your father is dead. He's been dead for two months. The sooner you come to terms with that, the better off we'll all be."

Awkward silence gripped the room. Bradley blinked at the shock of this personal affront. Tina glanced over at her father, desperate. He returned her look and nodded sadly, turning his attention back across the table.

"Eileen. Eileen, honey, look at me."

Her brow lined in deep furrows, Eileen finally looked at her husband. Bradley's head tilted and his eyes welled wet with tears.

"I'm so sorry," he said.

Eileen swallowed dryly, attempting to maintain any semblance of composure she might have had when the evening began. "Well. Thank you, Bradley, but it's a little too late for that."

Tina smiled, reaching out to grasp her mother's hand, connecting the two of them through her own touch. "Mom, at least the two of you are communicating. That's a step."

Bradley frowned. "I don't know what happened. That night is a blur."

Eileen blinked away her own tears and gave Bradley a sober look. "You were on your way home from Portland and were killed by a jackknifed eighteen-wheeler."

Tina sighed. "Mother. You can't remain in denial."

The table was silent as a realization washed over Eileen. Her eyes suddenly widened in panic and fear. "Oh, God."

Bradley reached across the table to take Eileen's free hand in his. "Do you remember?"

"Oh, God," Eileen croaked from a mouth drier than any arid desert. "We. *We* were on our way home from Portland. *We* were killed by that truck."

Bradley gave her hand a loving squeeze. "I'm so sorry."

For the first time in months, Eileen looked across the table at her husband without a barrier of guilt, or anger, or blame. "Oh...no, it wasn't your fault. Oh, honey..." She shifted her hand to reciprocate his grasp.

"I miss you," he said.

"I miss you too," she said.

Tina smiled through a veil of tears. "I miss you both. So much."

Bradley and Eileen turned to their daughter, the incalculable weight of denial lifted.

"It's okay, honey," he said. "We're not going anywhere."

Eileen turned to him. "Bradley," she said, advising in a motherly tone, "I think we have to."

Bradley frowned, gazing blankly at the table. It was clearly not his favorite option. "We can't stay?"

Eileen sighed. "We kind of got sidetracked. But it's time we completed the journey."

Tina squeezed each of their hands and released them. She took a deep breath and nodded. "She's right. You need to go."

Eileen beamed proudly. She knew her daughter would be okay.

Bradley sensed it too, and nodded in agreement—with one caveat: "Let us stay with you one more night. I want to do one thing."

૪૦

Eileen and Bradley sat, slumped on a couch in a typical suburban living room, their daughter Tina sandwiched between them. All three dressed in t-shirts and pajama bottoms, the shifting light of the television screen washing over them as they watched Roy Scheider sink closer to the ocean on the *Orca*'s mast.

Bradley nudged his daughter gently in the ribs. "Tina totally gave Brody this plan."

"I did," Tina grinned.

Bradley pointed as the shark crested the water, exposing the SCUBA tank in its wobbling maw. "See now, here he goes..."

Bradley and Tina shared a high-five as they recited along with the film, "Smile, you son of a bitch," and watched the shark explode into a wet, chunky mass.

Eileen chuckled, shaking her head. "Oh, you two..."

She and Bradley hugged Tina between them.

"Love you, honey," said Bradley.

"You're gonna be just fine," said Eileen.

Tina wiped away tears as she continued staring straight ahead at the television. "I know," she sniffed.

"And thank you," Eileen said.

"For everything," Bradley added.

Her parents stood, and her mother bent over to plant a kiss on her head. "We love you."

Then they were gone, and Tina sat alone on the sofa, staring absently at the screen, her face frozen somewhere between happiness and loss.

"I love you too."

℀

Originally written in 2013 as the script to an unproduced short film, a vehicle for three Seattle actor friends. I often process my own grief through art, especially writing. This was one such outlet.

The Spirit Was Willing

ೞ

It was New Year's Day, 1927, and the last thing Detective Sergeant Peterson expected to find at the grave site of Meredith Langston was... Meredith Langston. The recently-buried corpse lay slumped against the marble headstone, eyes shut, makeup as fresh as when they'd put her in the ground four days previous. The gown she'd been buried in was undamaged, sentimental jewelry still present and accounted for.

Two questions Sergeant Peterson had was how she'd come to be there, and why? The grave site was otherwise pristine; not an ounce of dirt had been moved. The unmolested state of the corpse seemed to indicate this was not a grave robbery. If it was a prank, it was in poor taste, but extremely well-executed. And why did the body of a noted San Francisco philanthropist decide to show up above ground the very morning her grandson—recently home from Stanford for the funeral—had disappeared from his bed?

It took Peterson the rest of the day to get the court order to exhume Meredith Langston's casket. The evening shift had just come on duty and Peterson knew it would be another all-nighter for him. He didn't know what he was expecting to find in what should have been an empty coffin, but it sure wasn't the dead body of Charles Langston, the missing college boy.

Times like these are usually when I get a phone call.

My name is Jim Holland, and if you saw me on the street, you probably wouldn't look twice. I'm the kind of guy who can disappear in a crowd. "Nondescript," as Peterson is fond of saying. Five-foot-nine, pale complected from living nocturnally, hair and eyes the color of mud, and usually a day behind on my shave. I wear the same gray suit every day, and the tie usually hangs loose. I smoke too much.

My partner, Mandy Hart, is my opposite in most every way. A tall, slim Creole gal from New Orleans with skin of deep cocoa, keen fashion sense and discerning amber eyes that can scan a person's soul and peer deep into the spirit world. In all my years of exposing frauds and charlatans, Mandy's the only true psychic I've ever encountered. And her legitimate skills have come in extremely handy.

"Happy New Year," Peterson greeted through the phone. I could already tell he wasn't too pleased with it. Then he explained the part about someone who should have been buried not being buried and someone who should be alive being buried where the first person wasn't buried, and before I'd even lit a cigarette, Mandy was standing by the office door with my coat and hat.

By the time we got to Laurel Hill, the cops had already wrapped both Langstons and packed them in an ambulance for their trip to the morgue for an autopsy. Peterson was pacing up and down in front of a row of headstones, lit cigarette wobbling in his lips as he muttered to himself.

"Nice night for a stroll through a graveyard," I greeted.

Peterson shook my hand, then Mandy's. I could tell she was already picking up a scent off the place.

"Show me the Langston grave?" she requested.

Sergeant Kenneth Peterson of the SFPD was close to six-foot-five with a chest like a bootlegger's barrel. He was impossible to miss, silhouetted against the encroaching fog—even on such a dark, moonless night. The orange falloff from his cigarette gave his face a vaguely nefarious look. He led us to a plot where several uniformed officers and cemetery workers stood around a now-dormant steam shovel. The whole place was a criss-crossed tartan of flashlight beams.

Mandy immediately wandered over to examine the coffin and the hole it had recently been liberated from.

"So let me see if I've got your story straight," I said to Peterson. "Mrs. Langston passed away... the 28th, was it?"

"The 28th. Tuesday," he confirmed.

"And the funeral was yesterday, on the 31st?"

"That's right."

"And when was Charles Langston reported missing?"

"This morning. Missing from his bed. No signs of forced entry or struggle."

"And also this morning..." I pointed at the open grave.

"Mrs. Langston was discovered next to the headstone. Six feet of earth, undisturbed." Peterson scratched his receding hairline and probably contemplated taking the vacation he never seemed to get. "We dug up her casket and found Charles Langston's body inside."

"So it's the ol' corpse switcheroo," I said, lighting my own cigarette.

"Except Chuck wasn't a corpse when he was put in the coffin," Mandy said matter-of-factly as she rejoined us away from the grave site.

"Chuck?" I asked.

"That was what he went by," she said casually.

"Actually, that's true," Peterson confirmed. "From what the family told us."

A lot of supposed "psychics" are earnest in their demeanor, needing constant validation that their statements are correct. Mandy isn't earnest. She just smiles and goes on her way, confident in her certitude.

"So what are we looking at, Holland?" Peterson squinted and the soft, orange light on his face went out as he dropped his cigarette to the ground and stepped on it.

I honestly didn't know what to say. It's not like this stuff is in the encyclopedia. We spend so much of our time debunking fake psychics and paranormal events, when the real stuff pops up, we often haven't a clue how to react.

"Well, I could take some shots with one of our special cameras, see if they pick up anything, but I'm more inclined to hear what Mandy has to say."

And boy, did Mandy have something to say.

"This is a new kind of entity I've not encountered before," she said. And that meant something, given her childhood steeped in the haunted past of New Orleans. "It has the ability to move matter through the astral plane."

Peterson shook his head. "How do you figure?"

"You've seen the result with your own eyes," she answered with a cryptic smile. "The entity feeds on the psychic energy of the victim, which is heightened at the moment of death. Add terror to the mix and you have an exponential release of such energy—it's a feast for this...thing."

I followed Peterson's lead and stomped out my cigarette on the ground. "So there's something... some kinda psychic vampire... taking living people and blinking them into graves, then removing the previous occupant, just for kicks?"

"Not for kicks," Mandy corrected, quite serious. "For food."

"I..." Peterson began, trailing off as he shook his head.

I nudged him back to the case at hand. "Sarge. This isn't your first dance. You helped us with the Noe Valley portal and solved the Jade Demon murders in Chinatown with Danny Long."

"That doesn't exactly make any of this *normal.*"

"Fellas," Mandy said gently, stepping between us. "We will need to keep a wary eye on the local cemeteries in the coming days. This may not be a spirit of human origin, but it has a taste for fear, and I think we will see more of these 'displacements'."

"Okay, Mandy," I nodded. "Let's play this smart. You consult with Oscar, see if you can't figure out a way to fight it. I'll check with the coroner and make sure this is what we think it is."

"And the P.D.?" Peterson asked, rubbing his jaw.

"Keep a detail stationed at every cemetery in town. The moment a corpse shows up out of the ground, you dig up that grave, pronto. Chances are good you could save a life."

Early the next day, we called on the city coroner, who had examined both   Langston corpses. Mandy had called our licensed mage consultant, Oscar Morgan, but there was no answer, so she decided to tag along with me and we could both see Morgan later.

The morgue was in the basement of an old brick building which had somehow survived the '06 quake and subsequent fire. It smelled like formaldehyde and a peculiar kind of body odor—the kind that shows up after weeks of not taking a bath. The kind one might try to mask with rose oil or fresh-cut flowers.

Doc Sawyer—his real name, I kid you not—was a short, bald man of 55 with spectacles and a bushy mustache. He had already done his examination of the two bodies, which had been shut away into two of the new refrigerated drawers where they could be kept indefinitely.

"Meredith Langston, female, age 79," Sawyer said, reading from his written reports. "Nothing different about her body, save for a few days' worth of decay."

"The body was not messed with in any other way?" I asked.

"No sir," Sawyer answered with firm assuredness before continuing. "Charles Langston, male, age 23. Definitely died of suffocation, but the condition of his hands and fingers, corresponding to the damaged interior of the casket, indicates he was alive at the time of...placement...and tried to claw his way out."

"Horrible," Mandy shuddered, and we all silently agreed.

I jotted down some notes and pointed at Sawyer's clipboard. "Was there anything else?"

"Just the residue," he said, walking to a counter and grabbing a glass vial with a cork stopper. "Found around the young man's eyes, nose and ears. It's not nasal discharge, nor any human bodily fluid."

Sawyer handed me the vial and had me sign for it. Mandy knew instantly what it was.

"Ectoplasm," she announced.

Sawyer almost rolled his eyes, but then he remembered all the weirdness that had descended upon San Francisco in the past year and corrected himself.

We thanked the good doctor and left with a vial of spirit tissue and confirmation of the entity's M.O. At the phone booth outside Edie's on Market, I spent the nickel for a call in to Peterson's precinct downtown.

Peterson wasn't in, and he'd left no message. Another nickel bought me confirmation that Oscar Morgan was home, and would see us.

I got lost in my head as the trolley whisked us down Market to the Mission District. Mandy, too, seemed miles away. This was a different kind of case—the kind that becomes personal, whether you want it to or not. I was glad we were getting some help. Morgan was a well-traveled and "financially-secure" occultist and author, renowned for his expertise in ancient magics. He owned a Victorian townhouse a couple blocks away from the actual Spanish mission that was the neighborhood's namesake.

He met us at the door in a black and gold satin smoking jacket, hair slicked back with Murray's pomade. He was tan, his pencil-thin mustache was flawlessly trimmed, and he reeked of aftershave and exotic travel.

"James! Amanda! Do come in!" he greeted in a baritone so buttery smooth it even made *my* temperature spike.

"Oscar," Mandy replied, allowing him to kiss her hand. "It's been too long. When did you get back from Paris?" She was gracious, but clearly immune to whatever sex appeal Morgan had on display. I remember thinking that was just as well.

"Why, Amanda, I wasn't in Paris," Oscar protested. "I just returned from Shanghai on business."

"Oh, so the gentleman was a passenger on the ship?"

Now I was intrigued.

Oscar raised an eyebrow. "Why I'm sure I don't know what you—"

"I've encountered enough Parisian gentlemen in New Orleans to be able to pick up that particular scent anywhere in the world. My dear Oscar, he's all over your smoking jacket."

There was a tense silence, then Morgan cracked a wide smile. "Fair play, Amanda! You got me!" He waved us into the parlor and set out a tea service. "His name was Jacques and he was lovely. Would you like tea? I just made it. It's oolong."

We sat and drank Oscar's tea and I gave him the rundown: a corpse which should have been in the ground had been swapped with a live person who *shouldn't* have been in the ground, who had *become* a corpse. Then, I let Mandy run with the ball. She knew how to talk to Morgan. They spoke different dialects of a common language. They went on about various types of inter-dimensional entities, lobbing options back and forth like they were playing tennis. I counted the word "entity" spoken at least thirty times. They might have actually mentioned "ley lines" as well. Finally, given the M.O., they settled on an entity of non-human origin—that is to say, something that didn't originate on our plane of existence, and which had *never been* human. It wasn't a ghost or a lost soul; it was a malevolent psychic vampire with the ability to pop through dimensions as easy as hopping on the cable car.

And we all agreed it had to be stopped.

We realized we'd talked well past sunset and into the night. It was already 10 o'clock and I was famished. Morgan said he needed a bit of time to locate a certain component that he could turn into a helpful tool in our kit. We took our leave and headed back to the office—which was also our apartment—stopping for takeout at Chu's on the way.

We feasted on chow mein and Mandarin chicken and talked some more over a couple bottles of near beer. I fell asleep on the sofa, and Mandy in the armchair.

I dreamed I was searching through an enormous, empty mansion, in the dark. I knew Mandy was in danger, but everywhere I looked, I couldn't find her. I suddenly turned the corner and saw her at the end of a long hall—she was bound by tendrils of ethereal light, struggling to move, unable to cry out. I began to run toward her down the hall, keeping her in the beam of my flashlight.

And then the face appeared—vaguely human but definitely not of this world—with blurred features, skull-like, and a mouth full of dagger teeth. It popped up over her shoulder, grinning its terrible grin, and I could tell the tendrils of light belonged to the thing. It would feed on Mandy's psychic energy, and feed well. I yelled her name, running down the hall at an agonizingly slow pace. The entity grinned and leered at me, then my flashlight flickered and died.

At 5 a.m. the phone rang, sending a jolt through my body. I sat upright and grabbed the receiver from the candlestick. It was Peterson. They had another displaced corpse, and another victim. At another cemetery.

We called a cab and headed back downtown.

Calvary Cemetery lay southeast across Geary from Laurel Hill, and due east across Masonic from Ewing Field—where just last November I'd seen the Oakland Oaks football team crush my San Francisco Tigers 3-0.

Along Geary, from Arguello Boulevard to Baker Street, it was pretty much "Cemetery Central", with the Oddfellows, Masons, Calvary and Laurel Hill graveyards surrounding a multi-purpose sports arena. Hooray for the home team, but if you get slaughtered, we have you covered.

There had been a lot of talk about shutting down the graveyards within the city limits and moving the bodies out to increase the local property values, but so far the voters had said no. Even so, the new burials in the area were usually restricted to family crypts, or plots that'd been paid for years ago. The Jewish cemetery had already put a moratorium on new burials, so most of the newly deceased were sent to Colma or South City. This made the recent interments something a bit special.

It was a few minutes shy of dawn by the time our cab pulled up. A surly beat cop named Stubbs was on the lookout for us, and led us deep into the cemetery. Another crowd of uniformed officers and funeral home employees stood gabbing around another steam shovel, and we were treated to the sight of a dapper old gent in a black pinstriped suit splayed out unceremoniously next to an open hole. The casket had been dug up and lay open nearby, and the recently dead body of a young woman lay inside, staring up into eternity.

Peterson stalked toward us, orange light from his cigarette making his face into a gargoyle again. "Where you been? Sleeping?" he demanded.

"Happy to bill you overtime," I answered, unflinching. "Who are the stiffs?"

"The swell in the suit is Antonio Feri. Age 67 when he died last week."

"Why does that name ring a bell?"

"His nephew, Jerry, is a bootlegger." Peterson flashed a look that, even in the dark, I could tell was frustration at his failure to bring the entire criminal element in San Francisco to justice.

"Jerry Feri," I chuckled. "You can't write this stuff." Funny names aside, I was glad the Italian mafia hadn't infiltrated my beloved city. Yet.

Mandy was already standing over the open casket nearby. "Anita," she whispered. Her cocoa-brown fingers flitted over the corpse's face, closing the poor woman's eyes and collecting some greasy residue from inside the coffin lid. She scraped it into a glass vial much like the coroner's and stopped it with a cork, dropping it back into her handbag.

Peterson nodded, ambling over to the coffin. "Anita Scariso. Antonio's daughter. Age 35. Married to Alfredo Scariso. Also a—"

Before Peterson could finish saying "boot-legger", a well-dressed man in pinstripes, spats and a Longley bowler hat came pushing through the small crowd of police officers. He was clearly distraught and, upon seeing the woman in the casket, paced back and forth next to the open grave and shook with tears of anger and regret.

"Anita! What happened? What has happened here?"

Peterson was all business. Clapping one large hand on the man's shoulder, he offered a cigarette with the other. "Alfredo Scariso. Can you tell me where you and your wife were last evening?"

The bootlegger composed himself and finally stood still, taking the cigarette and nodding. "Anita and I had just returned from a gala luncheon at the Orpheum, but it was just champagne and hors d'oeuvres, so we decided to have an early supper in the kitchen."

"When was this?" Peterson asked, scribbling in his notebook.

"About 4:30 in the afternoon."

"When did Anita disappear?" Mandy asked quietly, eliciting a shocked look from Scariso.

"I—I'm not sure," he stammered. "No later than 5. I went to the cellar to bring up a bottle of wine, and when I arrived, she was gone. I searched the house and walked the neighborhood... I returned after an hour and took the car out in a wider search. After scouring the city, I returned home and have been waiting by the telephone since then."

I could tell Scariso was a tough guy by nature, so it was oddly endearing to see him tear up over his late wife.

"And we called you just before 5 a.m.?" Peterson noted, checking his watch.

"Yes," Scariso nodded, transforming suddenly into a mass of conflicting emotions. "How could this happen? And what are the police doing to find her killer? What are *you* doing, Sergeant?" Although he was shorter than Peterson by nearly a foot, Scariso puffed up on his toes and got within three inches of his face, cheeks dark red with fury. We could see the spittle fly.

I knew I'd regret it, but Peterson and I went way back, so I intervened. "Look, Mr. Scariso. We're dealing with a supernatural entity here. There's nothing the police—"

"You're the ghost hunters I heard about on the radio, eh?" he turned his attention on me, face red and eyes ablaze. "I got a lot of friends in this city, Mister Ghost Hunter. You find whatever did this to my Anita, maybe you get to call yourself my friend, *capiche*?" He made a show of straightening my tie just a bit too tightly, inferring what would happen should we be unsuccessful. So much for the city being mob-free.

Peterson was a statue. "Stubbs," he said in a clipped tone, "come take Mr. Scariso's detailed statement and make arrangements for the autopsy." As the surly cop approached to take care of the bereaved bootlegger, Peterson added, "Condolences, Mr. Scariso."

"Yeah, thanks," Scariso muttered as he walked away, turning back briefly to point at me. "I'll be keeping an eye on you, Mister Ghost Hunter."

"So we have a slightly better timeline to work from," I said to Peterson as Stubbs escorted Scariso away. "The wife disappeared sometime before 5 p.m. When was Mr. Feri's body found displaced?"

Peterson flipped a page in his notes and fished his pocket for another cigarette. I pulled one from my own jacket and lit both with a wooden match.

"About 3 a.m., a night watchman was making his rounds and apparently got the bejeezus scared out of him."

"So if our psychic vampire abducted Anita at about 5..."

Mandy knew where I was going and completed my thought. "The average person can survive five and a half hours inside a sealed casket."

Peterson swallowed. "And how do you know... Nah. Never mind."

"That means we're looking at a time of death before midnight," I said.

The Sergeant took a deep drag on his cigarette and looked right at me. "Time of death is only relevant in the matter of 'how fast can we dig up the grave after the corpse appears?' What's interesting to me is that the new victims are linked by blood."

"Not with each other," I argued.

"No, not with each other. With the previous occupant."

Mandy's eyes went wide. "It's using the family bloodline to find the location. Most entities we know of that shift between dimensions need to have seen or visited a location before. But it can't have seen the inside of these graves. So it's using the victim's ancestry as a map."

"Hey Mandy," I said, "my Uncle Mike is buried at Laurel Hill. I want you to know that in case I go missing."

Mandy smiled. "Your Uncle Mike has been dead for ten years. This entity needs a closer connection to point the way. Both Langston and Feri were buried within the past week."

"Yeah," I nodded. "Just the same..."

"I'll dig you up with my bare hands if I have to," she promised with a wink.

Peterson gestured at Mandy with his cigarette. "What does your, uh, *juju* tell you about this thing's limitations, if any?"

"Well, the cemeteries are close together," she began. "Where was Chuck abducted?"

Peterson consulted his notepad. "The Langston family home is in Pacific Heights. The Scarisos live in North Mission."

"Those are just a few city blocks away from each cemetery," I offered. "Maybe this thing doesn't have an unlimited range."

"It's found a convenient food source," said Mandy, making Peterson shudder. "As long as it can find new victims, it won't be letting up any time soon."

"We should get back to Oscar Morgan," I said. "See what he's come up with to help us catch this thing."

Peterson nodded. "You do that."

"Hey, Sarge," I added, "Post some uniforms around all four cemeteries and have those steam shovels ready to burn. That way we'll have a better chance of finding a displacement soon enough to save the buried victim."

"Yeah. And we'll have the precincts keep an ear on the switchboards for any missing person alerts."

Mandy touched Peterson's shoulder as we began to head back to the street. "The displacements will be recently interred, in plots purchased before the 1901 moratorium," she said. "And the victims will be adult blood relatives."

"Stop the presses," Peterson put up a hand and halted Mandy in mid-stride. "Why adult?"

A gentle look washed over Mandy's face as she explained. "Why, because this entity requires absolute terror when it feeds. And while a child might experience terror of the unknown, an adult will feel terror from *knowing* what is happening."

We left Sergeant Peterson alone in the graveyard, as a cold morning breeze blew in off the Bay. We hailed another cab and headed back to the Mission District, to Oscar Morgan's town home once again. As anticipated, he met us in that same gold smoking jacket and offered us freshly-brewed oolong tea. The man was only unstructured in his carnal proclivities; everything else, it seemed, was by-the-book. This visit, however, held a gift in store. As we were comfortably ensconced in Oscar's front nook, sipping proper tea from China, he disappeared into an office and returned with a small wooden box. Several phrases and symbols—what I figured to be arcane spells—had been burned into the wood, which was beautifully finished with walnut oil.

As he approached, Oscar gave us each a parental look of warning, before opening the box and allowing us to see the contents in the morning sunlight. Inside the box, on a bed of dark green velvet, was a curious transparent object. It resembled a stone or crystal, yet it was artificially round, as if it had been crafted, like a warped marble with a convex side and a concave side. About four inches in diameter, it drew the sunlight into it and seemed to glow on its velvet seat. Mandy reached for it, but began to swoon. Oscar closed the box and I reached over to hold Mandy upright.

"Whoa there," I said. "What's that all about, Morgan?"

Oscar grinned a broad, white grin. "It's a psychic lens," he explained. "The crystal absorbs psychic energy from the convex side, while the user remains behind the concave side."

Mandy nodded. "So we can trap the entity."

"Precisely," Oscar kept smiling. "It also allows the user to see through the lens into the astral plane."

"It's beautiful," I said. "So how do we use it?"

"I'll do it," Mandy jumped in. "I can draw the entity to me."

"Are you sure?" I hesitated. "That thing almost toppled you here at the table."

Oscar chuckled. "As long as she stays behind the concave side, it should be fine. And she's right—her psychic ability can summon the entity to her."

"Where did this come from?" I wondered aloud.

"I found it on an expedition in Arabia," he explained. "It took some time and a fair bit of training to be able to figure out its properties and how to control it. It's been sitting in my collection for the past six years. Glad it can be of some use to you and Sergeant Peterson in the meantime."

We offered Oscar Morgan some money for his psychic lens, which he refused. Then we said our goodbyes and headed home to the office.

With a belly full of roast beef on rye and a root beer or two, I passed out on the Murphy bed in the side office—shoes, hat and all. Mandy meditated, sitting quiet and still in the overstuffed armchair in the corner. The psychic lens lay on its velvet bed, box open.

I awoke to darkness. I tried to sit up but bumped my head and had to lay back down. Drawing my lighter from the inside breast pocket of my jacket, I flicked the lever, creating the small, amber flame which presently illuminated my surroundings. The silk bunting was a dead giveaway, no pun intended. I was in a casket, and when I called out, I could tell by the dull acoustics that the casket was underground. As much as I tried to maintain my cool, the truth is I've never been keen on tight spaces. I gave myself the privilege of a few punches to the lid's interior and a second shout, before deciding to conserve my air and hoping aid arrived soon. But then a face—that horrible, blurry skull—thrust itself through the casket lid above my own, glaring down on me with evil intent. I cried out in surprise, and the thing began to smile. It was more a grimace, or an approximation of a smile performed by someone with no emotional reference. The thrum of a beehive on high alert erupted within my head. The buzz became a ringing, and I became dizzy. I watched the face as it smiled its practiced smile, and the casket began to rattle and shake apart. I braced for the imminent cave-in. Then Mandy's face replaced the entity's cruel visage, and I realized I'd been dreaming.

"What's the scoop?" I asked, trying to be casual.

"You were dreaming of it, weren't you?"

"What do you mean?"

"Well, to be clear, you were out of your body. You were traveling."

I struggled to a sitting position, reached for my pack of cigarettes on the side table, and fished one out. "Yeah, so I was dreaming. So what?"

"Jimmy. Psychic energy is a two-way street. Your astral body was roaming while you slept, and that is where this spirit travels. You didn't just dream the encounter. You were there—just not in your physical body."

"Lucky me."

Mandy looked into my eyes. "It now has your scent. We're not safe. Neither of us."

"Yeah," I agreed. "So we need to end it." I rubbed my temple, head still buzzing. "Did I hear the phone?"

Mandy sighed and gave my neck a therapeutic squeeze. "It was Peterson," she said. "There's been a new displacement. Masonic Cemetery."

It wasn't until we exited onto the street that I realized how late it was. We hailed a cab and headed back to Cemetery Central. Mandy clutched the carved wooden box tightly to her.

We arrived to find six uniforms and three detectives, a steam shovel work crew and the cemetery night watchman, all standing around a corner plot. The Masonic cemetery had sat unused for twenty years, as there were no vacant plots and most Masonic families were already using the funerary facilities in Colma. Nobody had been interred in the last week, month or even year. It was just dumb luck that the watchman had discovered the skeletal remains of a George Lamont—dead since 1897—splayed out like a Halloween decoration next to his own headstone.

"This is a new activity," Mandy worried.

"Well it sure ain't the M.O. you suggested early this morning," Peterson agreed. "What's it doing dragging thirty-year-old bones out of the ground?"

"Maybe its feeding has been making it stronger, able to trace bloodlines back farther," Mandy suggested. "Or something else."

I had a hunch, but I wasn't sharing it just yet. It occurred to me that sometimes objects, and not genetics, could carry a psychic impression over a long period of time. It could be that an item which had once belonged to the displaced—a Masonic ring, perhaps—might be the ticket. If they dug up the victim and he or she was in possession of such an object, my hunch would be proved.

Mandy paced nearby, shaking her head in frustration. She even peered through the lens a few times, scanning our surroundings. Every now and again, she'd catch my eye and say, "nothing" under her breath. The steam shovel went to work, and within fifteen minutes, the casket lid was visible. A team of cops in shirt-sleeves surrounded the casket in the hole and Peterson ordered it opened.

Mandy and I stood at the top of the grave, peering down over the cops as they pried the pine lid away from the box to reveal its contents. It was empty. Mandy walked away, disgusted. "It knows."

A shudder ran down my spine as I realized the implication. "It pranked us!" I spat.

Mandy stopped in her tracks, her jaw set like stone. "It knows. It knows *us*. It knows we're onto it, and now it's strong enough..."

"To throw us a curve ball," I finished. "Just great."

Now I was mad. We had to find this thing. Find it and dispose of it. It had become a personal affront to my honor and reputation as a ghost hunter.

Peterson was already flagging one of the plainclothes detectives. "See if we can track down the family that belongs to Mr. Lamont here. Make sure there's been no abductions or disappearances. At the very least, maybe this thing's playing a game of round-robin—might've stashed a potential victim in a different grave or something."

I tapped the sergeant on his massive shoulder. "Hey, Sarge, we're gonna see if Mandy can pick up the scent. If you find a home address, leave a message for me at the precinct. I'll keep checking in."

"Alrighty," was his gruff reply. "Go to it. I've had enough of this thing, and I'm counting on you two to kick its behind back to whatever dimension it came from."

We headed out from the cemetery gate and hailed a cab. Mandy held the lens to her forehead and scanned the city with her intuition open and her eyes closed.

"Balboa," she said softly. "1625."

"1625 Balboa Street," I instructed the driver, and when I looked back at Mandy—she was gone.

The psychic lens sat undisturbed on the seat next to me. The cab door was closed. There was no way she could have fallen out without someone noticing, least of all, me.

"Driver! Stop!" I barked.

The cabbie hit the brakes and the hack screeched to a halt. I opened the back door, panicked. "Mandy!" I called out, but no reply came.

In a fit of desperation, I removed my fedora, grabbed the lens from the back seat of the cab and held it up to my forehead, clamping my eyes shut.

Nothing.

Turning slowly from west to east, I began to see impressions, shadows, like peering through an aquarium at a face on the far side. If this thing could see the spirit realm, it made sense that sweeping it along Cemetery Central would have yielded some ghosts. And boy did it ever. They mostly roamed back and forth on their hallowed ground, content to replay old conversations or messages to their loved ones. None paid any attention to me, and I continued my sweep south and east, back toward— *there!* Suddenly my mind filled with a picture so vivid it could have been a new Douglas Fairbanks movie.

I could see the lights of the city against the night sky. The view panned down and I could see Mandy's dress and new patent leather flats. It was as if I were her. Or rather, she was sending me the images and I was picking them up through the lens. I knew she was trying to give me all she could so I could get to her fast. At her feet lay a small, gold signet ring of some kind. Was that the Masonic symbol? The view tilted to the left: the silhouette of a giant bell. Then to the right: a Spanish adobe arch overlooking... Market Street? Only one location in the city with that particular view: Mission San Francisco de Asís—or "Mission Dolores", as it was commonly known. Specifically the bell tower of the new basilica.

I ducked back into the cab and slammed the door. "Mission Dolores," I ordered, "and step on it!"

The cab took off like a sprinter with a hotfoot, screaming down Geary and Arguello, down Stanyon through Golden Gate park. I kept the lens to my forehead, angled toward Mandy at all times. Occasionally the cab would have to swerve or hit the odd pothole, which disrupted my connection, and that separation filled me with a dread I'd never known. I couldn't lose her. Not now. Not like this. As we weaved down street after street toward the

Mission District, I kept getting glimpses of Mandy's situation—moving from arch to arch, looking for any egress, chased from the hatch and passage by a frenetic crackle of blue-white energy. She was trapped in the belfry, her only escape from the entity a fifty-foot drop to the pavement below.

And there it was.

The spirit from my nightmares, billowing like a sheet on a clothes line, snapping savage tendrils of ectoplasm. And the face. The sneering face of evil, an impish skull grinning blade-like teeth, eye sockets empty but for two tiny, glowing sparks—just inches from her own face. I could hear its thoughts, through Mandy and the lens. It had sensed her after the first killing, and as we came closer to discovering its true nature, it had used Mandy's psychic sensitivity like a convenient cable car, hitching a ride right to her physical body. The displacement of Lamont, the old Mason, was indeed a ruse. This dimension-hopping entity saw her not as a predator, but as a competitor. Of course either one meant it must be rid of her.

Glowing ember eyes burned into her psyche. Mandy tried to look away, to keep it from maintaining psychic contact with her, all the while trying to keep me connected, and that effort was exhausting her. It wouldn't be long before simply resisting the entity would prove too much, and she would plummet to her death, and it would feed.

I tossed a five into the front seat of the cab. It screeched to a stop in front of the basilica, but I was already out and sprinting across the sidewalk and up the front steps.

The entry was locked from the inside.

I jogged to the north side of the bell tower and called up to Mandy. All I could see was a strange, flickering blue light and a buzzing sound like a playing card stuck in an electric fan—just like the sound from my nightmare. I held up the lens and could see flashes of light and that sneering, snarling face. Then it looked at me—not at Mandy, but *through* her and straight into my head.

And then I was wrapped in tendrils of blue-white spectral energy, and my ears popped as we blinked away into nothingness, and reappeared in midair at the top of the bell tower. Mandy screamed from the arch facing me as I seemed to hover weightless for a split-second. Immediately aware of what was in store for me, I tossed the lens toward her, and she caught it. Then I felt gravity take over, and the ground rushed up at me. As I began to plummet toward the pavement, I caught the quickest glimpse of Mandy holding the lens to her forehead, eyes closed in the use of her power.

I heard an unholy scream from above, and my shoulder exploded in agony as my left hand snapped out and caught the wrought iron balcony railing of the first level. The pain dimmed for a moment as shock started to kick in, then it washed over me with a vengeance.

And there I dangled, thirty feet above the street, as a small crowd began to gather on the sidewalk. I knew I could survive a ten, maybe twenty-foot fall onto cement, but survival at thirty wasn't guaranteed, especially if I impacted the wrong way—ribs could puncture lungs, skull could crack open like a coconut. It felt like I was hanging there for hours, but was probably only a couple minutes at most. The fire in my arm radiated from my neck to the tips of my fingers, and I began to lose my grip as those same fingers began to go numb.

And I let go.

The next thing I knew, I was being hauled into the alcove by Mandy and a chubby priest with glasses who said his name was Father Paul. Mandy clutched me tightly and kept repeating, "we did it."

We did it, she said. *We did it.*

My arm stopped burning and everything went numb, and I passed out hard.

When I awoke at French Hospital two days later, my left shoulder and arm were in a cast and Mandy was sitting in a chair next to the bed.

"Morning, Jimmy," she smiled.

"You okay, doll?" All I could think of was the peril I'd last seen her in, and how much she meant to me.

My concern was met with a shy smile and the wave of a hand. "I'm fine."

I tried to piece together the fragments in my head, but finally had to ask what happened.

"You threw the lens to me," Mandy explained, "and I summoned the entity. It was so intent on killing me that it didn't hesitate, and I drew it in through the front of the crystal."

She adjusted my blanket and added, "I took it to Oscar and he's locked it away for safe keeping."

That didn't surprise me at all. Of anyone in the city, Oscar Morgan was probably the most reasonable choice to make sure that thing never got loose. And as long as Sergeant Peterson didn't have to deal with it anymore, I knew he'd be okay with that. Although I wasn't sure how he'd end up reporting this case. Then again, that was Peterson's job, not mine.

I noticed a large bouquet of flowers in a crystal vase in the corner, and immediately wondered if I was in the right room. "Nice flowers," I observed.

Mandy noticed my quizzical look. "They're from that fella, Scariso," she said. "Apparently we have a new friend."

Oh good, I thought. *Now we have the attention of a Sicilian family of bootleggers.* At least the attention, for now, was favorable. I hoped it would remain that way.

I tried to sit up, but the stabbing pain in my shoulder had other ideas.

"Uh uh," Mandy scolded, arranging the blanket around my chest. "You tore your pectoral muscle, dislocated your shoulder and fractured your collarbone."

"That's quite the laundry list," I said.

"They've got you on morphine for the pain, and you'll be in the cast for six weeks. So you might as well relax until they let me take you home."

Let me take you home, I thought. I liked the sound of that.

For what it was worth, 1927 was off to a great start.

An original contribution to the first AEGIS Tales retro pulp anthology from 2018. The characters actually date back to the late 1980s, when I was working on an "old spooky house" screenplay. Jim and Mandy appear in the *AEGIS Tales Radio Adventures* in an episode called "The Holland Agency."

Rendezvous Dogs

౪

Lance sat in an oak dining chair, peering out through his living room window in a quiet suburban home. Deep brown eyes glared from behind slim, fashionable glasses, a sliver of bright sunlight bisecting the dome of his shaved head in direct contrast to his dark skin tone. He was immaculately dressed in a tailored shirt, its collar open, under a Navy blue jacket and matching slacks.

He was almost a statue: still but for the gentle motion of the hairbrush.

Muffin lay across his lap, breathing contentedly as the brush in his hand caressed the length of her body. She was a canine of the Lhasa Apso variety, small and white, with a darling pink bow that kept her long hair from her eyes. Pearly teeth shone in an underbite; she was scant generations removed from wolves, now perfectly at ease in the lap of a human.

Outside, the local cat lady, Frieda, assailed the neighborhood with a handful of printed fliers and a staple gun. The bespectacled woman in her forties was squeezed into a powder-blue velour track suit a couple sizes too small, and carried an assortment of colorful streamers and jingle-bell toys to attract her quarry, which apparently had gone missing.

Lance and Muffin tracked her every step through the crack in the drapes, startling as she turned and caught their surveillance. Lance quickly stood from the chair and pulled the curtain closed, just as the mobile phone buzzed in his jacket pocket. Muffin hopped to the floor and retreated to the sofa.

"Hello?" Lance greeted, holding the phone to his ear.

The voice at the other end of the call was deep, stern and feminine. "Lance. It's Stone. The Boss wants to meet you."

Lance's face became a mask of fear. "I think Frieda saw me," he warned.

"We can't worry about that," Stone replied. "It's time to go."

Lance collected his wits, leaning close to the crimson drapery as he hissed, "But what if...they...find out?"

"You've come too far to be having second thoughts," Stone admonished. "Are you in or not?"

Lance put his eye close to the drape and edged it away from the window trim. He squinted past the sunlit front garden to the sidewalk, where Frieda stood—staring defiantly back at him.

He turned away from the window and let the curtain fall closed. With the phone to his ear, he nodded solemnly. "I'm in."

ℰ

Lance was just like every other well-dressed man over six feet in height, walking a tiny white dog along the sidewalk through town. The juxtaposition between them in mass and scale was totally normal and not the least bit comical.

Stone appeared from behind a mailbox, built like a power lifter, hair in a tight ponytail, dressed in boots, yoga pants and a leather jacket, with a matching dog at the other end of her leash. Spike had white fur and the same underbite as Muffin. He was the same size, with the same bulging brown eyes. The only thing denoting his gender was a small blue necktie.

Two large humans, out walking their identical dogs on a sunny afternoon. There was nothing at all suspicious about it. Their dark sunglasses, occasional furtive glances and nonchalant gait broadcast to the world that everything was absolutely, completely normal.

છ

As they crossed the threshold of where the sidewalk ended and made their way toward the wooded area of the public park, Lance continued to cast nervous looks over his shoulder. Stone led him along a path deeper into the woods, flagging him to a halt as she caught sight of the woman ahead.

Andrea was slender, pale-complected, and hair cut in a severe bob. She was dressed much like Stone, in black boots, yoga pants and a leather jacket. To Lance, it looked just like a uniform. He wondered how he'd look in yoga pants.

The Boss lay at Andrea's feet, a black Cairn terrier in a red service harness. He stared up at Stone as she approached, removing her glasses and cracking an excited smile.

"I brought him," Stone announced quietly.

Andrea looked past her to see Lance darting his eyes around their location nervously. "Proceed," she ordered.

Stone waved Lance ahead, beckoning him and Muffin to approach.

As Lance drew nearer, Andrea put up her hand, and he halted in mid-stride. She pointed two fingers at his eyes and flicked them in a downward motion. He understood, removing his sunglasses.

Andrea squinted at him. "Were you followed?"

Lance swallowed, his mouth dry. "I...no." An uncomfortable moment passed, and he added, "I don't think so?"

"You don't think so?" Andrea repeated, suddenly suspicious.

Stone glared. "He's being paranoid."

"You should get that looked at," Andrea suggested.

"I...what?" Lance's forehead wrinkled up like a prune.

Andrea sighed. "WERE YOU FOLLOWED?"

Lance summoned his composure. "No," he answered with gravitas.

"My name is Andrea. But my call sign is *Chew Toy*. You've already met Stone." A wry smile suddenly broke across her face. "I'll be your tour guide to the Insurgency."

℘

Andrea strode along the wooded path, gently cradling The Boss in her arms as one would hold a baby. Lance and Muffin followed a step behind, with Stone and Spike bringing up the rear.

"What do you know of the cause?" Andrea quizzed.

"The Dogs' Resistance?" Lance clarified. "It's a rebellion against the Feline Empire."

Stone frowned in disgust. "Cat people," she spat.

Andrea continued her recruitment pitch. "We need like-minded canines and their human symbiotes to take down the feline oppressors," she explained. They stopped in mid-stride, Andrea finding Lance's gaze. Spike and Muffin exchanged a quiet glance, and Andrea took a step closer to Lance. "Stone thinks you're up to the task. So what do you say? Are you willing to fight?"

Lance paused as if searching the well of his very soul for an answer, but he already knew what the answer would be. "I..." he began, not noticing that a red laser point was roaming across his broad forehead.

Andrea and Stone saw it, however, instantly panicking until they turned to see Frieda, holding a small laser pointer and a loose poster showing her lost cat.

All three humans turned toward Frieda, followed by all three dogs.

"Sorry," Frieda chirped, turning off the laser and lowering it. "Um...have you seen Captain Fluffypants?" The poster clutched in her hands read *HAVE YOU SEEN ME?* above a large portrait of a white Persian cat.

The three compadres only stared, as did the dogs.

"Well?" Frieda repeated. "Have...you?"

Suddenly a deep voice growled seemingly out of thin air. It was The Boss, the Cairn terrier in the service harness, focusing his mental powers into language humans could understand. "Captain Fluffypants has been...replaced" he announced.

Frieda was instantly distraught. "Replaced? No! Not Captain Fluffypants!" She backed away into the trees as the dog people began to push in.

Andrea's face became maniacal. "Release your feline affinity," she ordered.

"Become one with the canine," Lance added.

Stone squinted, cutting off the last point of access to the park path. "Join the movement."

Spike and Muffin pressed forward. "ONE OF US," they chanted. "ONE OF US."

The Boss laughed in a guttural display of pleasure as Frieda cringed against the trunk of a tree, clasping her hands over her ears and dropping the poster to the wooded path. "BE-GIN THE MIND MELD," he instructed.

Clamping her eyes shut in terror, hands gripping her head like talons, Frieda let out a long, primal scream, and then everything went dark.

ൈ

The girl sat up excitedly in bed. This had been the most riveting bedtime story she'd ever heard in all of her six years. Gripping the comforter in two tiny fists, she leaned forward with wide blue eyes, her chestnut hair in braided pigtails, stuffed animals rolling into the depression she'd left.

"But what happened?"

The Boss lay at the foot of the girl's bed, storybook open flat in front of him. He found her gaze with his dark terrier eyes and said, "They all lived happily ever after."

ൈ

Written in 2017 as a short film script. The headhopping and switching of sympathies is intentional, keeping the reader off-balance on this bonkers ride into a world where dogs have overthrown cats as the authority in charge of humans.

Still Life

ℛ

The woman paced nervously in front of the crib, biting her nails and red in the face. Tears gathered in her swollen eyes and began to leak down her jaw, wetting her loose night shirt in dark streaks. She tried to breathe through a nose clogged with apprehension and emotion, which did nothing but make a pitiful sucking sound in the eerily quiet apartment.

The man approached quietly from the other room, padding across the hardwood floors in his socks and pajama pants, t-shirt loose around his waist. A day's growth of beard was already visible on his face, which became a mask of concern as he came to a stop at the woman's side.

He peered into the crib and recoiled when he saw what had made the woman so incredibly upset.

The baby wasn't moving.

It lay silent and still, no breath or motion,

no cries out of hunger or discomfort.

Absolute stillness.

The man wasn't sure where to begin. "What—what happened?"

The woman pressed her hands to her temples, trying to recall something. "Did I forget? I'm not entirely sure…"

"How long has it been?" asked the man, leaning over the crib rail for a better look. He reach in, pulling back the soft knit blanket to reveal the baby, unmoving.

"I don't know," the woman shook her head, sobs rushing into her throat once more. "I thought it might have been my day, but…I don't remember."

The man's brow arched up in the middle, as it always did when employing empathy. "It's going to be okay," he said, pulling the woman closer. He caressed her shoulder, repeating, "It's going to be okay."

"But what if it was my fault?" the woman demanded. "I don't think I could live with myself."

"We'll get through this," said the man.

"How do you know?"

"We always do."

The woman hugged her arms around her body as the man pulled away and went to the dresser in the corner of the room.

"I don't know," she worried. "It may have been too long."

"No use losing ourselves in the abyss until we know all is truly lost," the man said, as if preaching some great cosmic truth from a church pulpit. "Besides, I think this was on me."

The woman's face suddenly went pale. "What?"

"I don't think you forgot," he said. "I remember now. It was my day."

"H—How," she stammered, "how could you just...forget?"

"I know," the man sighed in defeat. "It's not like me at all."

"You are so good about remembering," the woman fretted, "when it's my time, or your time. How could you forget *our child?*"

"Yes," answered the man, digging through the top drawer in the dresser. "I know. I accept full responsibility."

The woman saw that he was searching for something, and it piqued her curiosity. "What are you looking for?"

"We usually keep it in the top drawer, yes?"

"It depends on what you're talking about."

"You know what I'm talking about."

"Do I?"

"I think you do."

The woman folded her arms across her chest. She was more than a little angry with him now. "Yes, it should be in the top drawer."

The man rummaged around under a stack of folded onesies, finally grasping the object in question. "Aha, he said, relieved. "I found it."

He returned to the crib and glanced over the side. The child had not moved position, nor drawn a breath. It was still rigid, unmoving, and absolutely silent.

"I'm sorry I forgot," the man said. "I won't forget anymore."

Reaching down into the crib, he gently stroked the child's back, feeling for the switch. He knew it was in the mid-thoracic vertebrae, somewhere around T6. He found it on the fourth try, pushing it down like a toggle. There was an almost inaudible click as the skin retracted over T8 and T9, revealing a round slot.

Producing the object he'd found in the drawer, the man inserted what appeared to be an antique skate key into the opening. He twisted it carefully clockwise, listening to the gears and springs as they ratcheted into place, mindful of over-winding the mechanism.

When he felt the tension was optimal, he removed the key and gently flipped the toggle switch, closing the spinal access port.

Then he backed away, standing next to the woman as they both gazed down into the crib, waiting...

A series of rolling clicks and pings became audible from within the body of the tiny child, and suddenly its diaphragm expanded in a breath. Small, chubby legs and delicate arms began to wiggle, and the baby's over-sized head popped up, eyes blinking in the soft morning light.

It began to coo and smile, pushing itself up on its tiny arms.

The woman reached down and scooped up the infant, kissing its forehead and bouncing it softly in a motherly dance.

"Let us never forget to wind the baby," she admonished in a whisper.

The man closed his eyes and nodded. "Never again." He went to the dresser and returned" the key to its place beneath the stack of folded onesies.

The baby giggled and sighed, cradled in the woman's arms.

∞

Original concept dates back to about 1991, as a wish-fulfillment fantasy resulting from the loss of my baby brother to an accidental overdose in 1972. Over the years, this story has taken on new meaning. It shows how partners can go to extremes shouldering far more than their rightful share of the emotional burden from such loss, and how we really depend on each other for basic survival.

Lunch

(A Psychological Comedy)

෨

Brent sat quietly in the booth between the two women, trying to read the menu. A rendering of the moon's face scowling with the rocket lodged in its eye stared back at him. Cafe Méliès served a famously-delicious selection of nouveau cuisine with the occasional greasy-spoon favorite thrown in to appeal to the hangover crowd. And that described this trio to a T.

A square-jawed man of some 30 years, Brent wore a collared shirt-tie-and-hoodie combo favored by local hipsters. His dark hair sprouted uncombed from his skull, his face a bristly mask of lost sleep and lack of a razor.

Madison sat on his right, a boisterous brunette in a black cocktail dress, also perusing the menu. Her lipstick and mascara blurred on her pale features, worn from hours of abuse without a touch-up. Shelly sat across from her on Brent's left, dressed almost identically to Madison, and yet far more put together. Her dark hair was styled, her makeup tasteful and neatly applied. Her eyes weren't even the least bit puffy.

If all of them had been out partying until the wee hours, Shelly was the only one with plausible denial.

The three sat in awkward silence as the cafe bustled around them with activity and chatter. Brent hoped today would be different. He hoped they could just have lunch in peace, and not do the thing. The thing they always ended up doing.

Shelly finally broke the silence. "What are you thinking?"

Brent winced. Shelly had fired the first salvo. She'd invited Madison to speak. This could only get worse.

Madison kept her eyes buried in her menu, but her words flew with surgical precision. "That you dressed the same as me. Again."

Shelley continued to read from her own menu, not agitated at all by the comment. "No, to eat."

Brent glanced at Madison. There was still a chance. Shelly had deflected the sour line and was trying to keep a civil tone.

"Not sure," Madison chirped, almost

sweetly. "Something fatty and carb-laden, that represents my extreme level of self-loathing." Madison actually glared at Shelly with the last part of the comment, as if inviting a violent response. It was the conversational equivalent of the Bruce Lee "come at me, bro" gesture.

"Stop," Shelly frowned, giving Madison a maternal, disappointed look. "What kind of talk is that?"

"Same talk as always," Madison replied, chin out, daring Shelly to take a physical swing, let alone a metaphorical one.

"Well you shouldn't do it," Shelly lectured, dropping her gaze back to the array of food items described in front of her.

Madison saluted almost comically. "Yes ma'am!"

Silence once again descended on the table, the three nervously reading their menus. Brent silently prayed there would be no further discussion. He just wanted to have lunch and get out of there.

"...not healthy," Shelly muttered.

Oh God, thought Brent. *They're going to do the thing.*

Madison dropped her menu to the table. "I know it's not healthy. That's what makes it so good."

Shelly met her gaze across the table. "Are you still talking about food?"

"Are you not?" Madison quizzed.

"I'm talking about mental and emotional health, Maddie."

Madison bristled at the shortened moniker. "Madison."

"What?"

"I fucking hate that nickname," Madison leered, eyeing Shelly with laser-focused intensity. "My name is Madison."

Brent looked at Shelly to make her next move. Shelly was a pro at the passive-aggressive shrug-off, and that's precisely what she did.

"I'm sorry," she chimed, returning her focus to the menu.

But Madison wasn't finished. "What the hell is 'Shelly' short for, anyway?"

Brent frowned. She was going to push this. But how far?

"Michelle? Rachelle? Tortoise shell?"

He watched as Madison flung abuse from her side of the table, impressed as Shelly dodged each word without so much as shifting in her seat. It was not unlike watching talented dancers. Or acrobats. Or MMA fighters. Or an unholy amalgam of all of them.

Shelly looked up from her menu, batting her eyes innocently. "Never really thought about it. I've always just been Shelly."

Brent breathed a labored sigh of relief. Maybe they wouldn't do the thing after all. Perhaps the thing had been avoided.

Madison squinted. "You know, that was perfectly good bait. But not only do you not take it, you completely ignore the fact that I'm taunting you."

Shelly kept her eyes on the menu. "I know you're taunting me. It's what you do. It's your constant state." Delicately turning the page, she added, "Mine is taking the high road."

Brent winced in trepidation. That was a jab born of a lifetime of sharpening the very implements of jabbing. The thing was, in fact, happening. He wasn't sure they would last through lunchtime, let alone the rest of the day, or beyond.

Madison laughed viciously. "There's taking the high road, and there's being obtuse."

"Refusal to take the bait," Shelly asserted, "is not the same as being obtuse."

Brent nervously cleared his throat.

Madison and Shelley took notice of the man between them for the first time.

"Touche," said Madison, returning to her menu. "I'm sorry."

Shelly put on a pleasant face. "Maybe we should just decide on what to eat."

Brent relaxed, but the calm was short-lived.

"I'm really craving...chicken and waffles!" Madison squealed, flush with excitement.

Shelly ignored her. "Ooh, salmon and quinoa with steamed vegetables."

"Or maybe," Madison countered, "chicken and waffles!"

The two women locked eyes across the table and Brent sat flush with the seat, trying to stay out of the line of fire.

"Vegetables," Shelley said.

"Waffles!" demanded Madison.

"Quinoa."

"Waffles!"

"Quin—"

"Waffles!"

"Madison—"

"Motherfucking waffles," Madison sang like a 1960s Motown star.

Silence returned and Brent glanced around the restaurant to see if anyone had taken notice, but the cafe patrons were buried in their own lunches, preoccupied with their own drama.

Shelly extended an olive branch. "Maybe Brent should decide."

Both women turned to look at Brent, and he slouched into the cushion, embarrassed at the attention.

Madison was dismissive. "Brent should

decide? Why should Brent get to choose for us?"

"Because he's picking up the tab," Shelly retorted as if the "duh" was implied.

"So?"

"So? So he should at least decide for himself."

Brent discovered if he tried to slouch any lower, he was in danger of sliding under the table, which might actually have been preferable to his current situation.

Madison became indignant. "I'm sorry? Um, have you forgotten that *we're* the ones calling the shots here?"

Shelley tried to maintain her composure. "We're only *part* of the equation..."

"Have you forgotten," Madison continued, clearly on a roll, "that we've always made these decisions?"

Shelly rolled her eyes. "You're so frustrating..."

"From what to eat, to what's attractive..."

"So full of yourself..."

"And even that one boy, in 9th grade shop class—"

If Shelly had a line, Madison had finally crossed it. "Goddamnit, Madison! This isn't about your fucking power trip!"

Brent watched as Madison made the

motion of pushing up nonexistent sleeves. She was ready to brawl.

"Oh? Do tell..."

As if clipping the fuse to a bundle of TNT, Shelly suddenly softened her tone, and, returning to her calm, maternal demeanor, smiled at them both. "This is about doing what's best for all of us."

But Madison wouldn't be satisfied with that. "And maybe," she argued, "sometimes that means not doing what's best, huh? Moderation in all things, including moderation?"

Shelley stared blankly at Madison like a deer in headlights. "Fine," she said, her voice barely above a whisper. "Order the chicken and waffles. And we can cry ourselves to sleep tonight. Alone. Again."

Madison knew Shelly had made a fair point, but couldn't let it go. "Whatever," she muttered, looking away.

Shelley pressed on, calm and focused, choosing each word for its surgical sharpness. "Because nobody wants to date a flabby loser with no self-respect."

"Wow," Madison glared. "Don't mince words, Shelly."

Brent scowled.

Shelly's look was pleading, but her words were savage. "Well I wouldn't have to go on the war path if you weren't so goddamned out of control."

"I'm out of control?" Madison gasped. "Who threw the hissy fit in the bar last night and totally wrecked any chance to score?"

Shelly leaned forward, squinting. The gloves were off. "If you hadn't been pouring endless Jaeger shots—"

Brent's hands had slammed down on the table before he knew what was happening. "Enough!" he bellowed, unconcerned about being overheard.

Madison and Shelly startled, eyes wide, mouths agape as Brent gripped the table and leaned forward with more intensity than they'd ever seen him muster.

"I am sick to death of you two tearing all of us down, as you sink your claws into each other in the name of doing what's best." He threw a serious, parental look at each of the women. "It doesn't have to be all one way or the other. If we want chicken and waffles, we can have chicken and waffles." He let the words sink in, then added, "We'll just have to work out twice as much this week."

Shelly and Madison looked at each other, chastened and sheepish.

"Extra gym time is good," Shelly offered quietly.

Brent smiled. "Point, Ego."

Both turned to look at Madison, who adjusted the bodice of her dress with an almost haughty demeanor.

"If it means the possibility of getting lucky this weekend," she said, "I'm in."

Brent nodded at her. "Point, Id. And my vote as Superego makes it unanimous." He leaned forward, glaring at each of his companions. "Now, can we please eat?"

The women looked at each other, then back at Brent. Finally they relaxed, returning to their menus.

ॐ

Paula finished a bite of waffle and pushed the plate away, perplexed. Sandy hair pulled back in a ponytail, she'd left her purple hoodie unzipped enough to reveal a black Lycra sports bra underneath.

Time to get to the gym, she thought, adjusting the glasses on her nose and dropping some extra dollar bills into the check tray on the table. Slinging the strap of her small purse over her shoulder, she slid out and exited the busy cafe, leaving an empty, silent booth behind.

ॐ

Written in 2013 as the screenplay for the short film of the same name for three of my favorite Seattle actors, featured at the Seattle Shorts Film Festival 2014.

Old Lazarus

୨୦

The first time he saw the old man, he'd taken him for a mugger. Or at the very least, some half-crazed renegade subject from the UW psychology department. The figure had stood, just inside his peripheral vision, long black duster whipping across the tops of his cowboy boots in a simile of bat wings. His dark, Native hair, stringy and streaked with an ancient gray, hung roughly to his shoulders when it wasn't being blown about beneath the black bolero with a glint of silver and turquoise from the hat band.

That had been two nights ago. Downtown, the corner of Fifth and Denny, near the Space Needle.

He was back tonight. Different part of town, same Indian.

Mark Crowell could only stare. His vision was marred by the stinging wind and accompanying splats of cold rain on his glasses; nonetheless, he stood with legs like pitons sunk into the concrete of Pioneer Square. Wrapping his coat a bit tighter against the blustery January night, the artist blinked the rain and his own saline from blue-gray eyes and looked again: perhaps hoping that the gaunt, nightmarish apparition was a wandering vagrant, or better yet, some hallucinatory manifestation of the deep-fried seafood combo plate he'd consumed for lunch.

No dice.

The figure was quite solid, coattails flapping, the stare of ancient eyes searing into his skull. Mark shuddered, counting paces to the gallery. Liz would be closing up now, and he knew for a fact that two people had a much slighter chance of being accosted than one person. But still his feet refused to budge—he remained bonded to the slick pavement, shaggy blond hair matted by wind and rain... helpless except to stare mindlessly at the figure in the shadows.

What nearly made him soil his jockeys was the way the old man spoke directly into his brain without so much as moving his lips; in fact, the voice was barely a whisper, thus Mark's immediate thought was that it must be the wind howling down the avenue...

But then again, the wind didn't usually hiss:

...*beware.*

"Aww, man. I don't need this shit." Mark turned away from the apparition across the square. The soft glow of neon shop fronts led the way down First Street, the muffled bashing of waves along the waterfront urging him out of the dark. He squinted through the rain again at the old Native. The stranger's words were thick and cracked, like dried mesquite buried in warm sand.

...*beware.*

"Beware what?!" Mark was beginning to get pissed.

beware the chameleon.

"Uh, right. Thanks. I'll remember that." He blinked again, suddenly aware of the feeling returning to his legs and feet. He scanned the shadows across the square one last time, but the old man was no longer there—only a big raven, probably blown off course by the storm front, pushing, flapping hard against the wind as it winged upward, out of view.

&

The gallery was locked, dim security lights limned his face from inside. He knocked again. "Shit." What was her problem? They'd agreed to meet at the gallery after closing, as was their usual Friday night custom. It wouldn't be the first time she'd left without him, but given the recent string of eerie Indian sightings he'd had, it seemed to irk him just that much more. Why tonight, of all Friday nights? And what of his work? Mark Crowell shrugged his wet shoulders and turned away from the gallery window. This meant one of two things: either she'd sold his painting and was home changing to surprise him and take him out for a night of celebrating, or she hadn't sold the piece as anticipated, and was home drinking, trying to manufacture a good sob story and lots of sympathy.

In either case, she was home.

He backed away from the storefront, jammed his hands deep into his pockets and headed up to the bus stop on Third. Just stay where it's light, he told himself, and the ravens and the bogeymen and the old Indians won't get you.

The piercing, unearthly call of the same damn lost raven jarred his mind back into the giant vat in his consciousness marked *FEAR*. He could hear the damp flap of wings through the rumble of cold wind past his ears. His head sunk down further into the woolen safety of his raincoat, and he slouched forward as he sped his pace toward the bus.

Good bus. Wonderful bus. He'd be safe on the bus.

The rolling steel shelter was already stopped, releasing its scurrying cargo like baby spiders from the egg-sack. Mark stepped inside, flashed his transit pass. The abrupt hiss of brakes releasing made him jump, but he managed to take his seat near the driver as the vehicle pulled away. He scanned the interior: a handful of ragged mothers, shift workers, and a goateed musician in motorcycle leather and denim.

Mark Crowell blinked but this time it felt like more of a nervous twitch. The old Native sat in the far rear of the transit bus, his cold steel gaze peering out from the wet brim of the hat. The inside temperature dropped sharply, or maybe it was Mark's blood going ice cold. He looked away quickly.

...*beware the chameleon.*

Mark cringed. There was that desert voice again, dry and deep in his head. This time he answered back in kind: with his own mind.

Alright. Fine. Thank you. I promise I'll beware the chameleon. Now please leave me alone. I have enough to worry about.

maybe more than you think.**

What?

if you want to live, bilagáana, do what I tell you.**

Mark looked back, and in the old Indian's place sat a portly man in a raincoat and fedora, poring over the sports news in the Times. Somehow, the artist wasn't surprised at what he saw. An absurd, jaded acceptance flushed through him and he caught himself midway through a nervous chuckle.

What could he possibly have been thinking? Why would the bus be any safer than, say, a morgue?

∞

The long fifth floor corridor of the apartment building indeed reminded him of a mortuary: the endless red carpet, tables with fresh irises every two doors or so. He found Liz's unit, number 513, rang the buzzer. Her voice was like a bright ray of salvation through the door.

"Who is it?"

Mark allowed himself a smile. "It's me."

"Me who?"

"Stripping candy-gram."

"Oh, by all means, come in."

He entered, and she met him with an enthusiastic kiss. His stress level melted away, and he was finally able to let his shoulders fall. "Good news, I hope."

The pretty brunette grinned, brown eyes bright with excitement. "Oh, Mark. Wonderful news!"

careful, bilagáana.

Mark's smile dropped, and he suddenly noticed how unusually dark the room was. His gaze shot past his lover to the curtained window where the old man's silhouette stood solid and black. Completely still.

"What the fuck?!"

Liz glanced over her shoulder, her eyes showing surprise more than fear. "Mark, who is that?"

"Some crazy old geezer who's been following me around all night." The words were grim, angry, and he carefully moved Liz aside so that he faced his dark nemesis. "And, to tell you the truth, he's really starting to piss me off."

"I have that affect on people," was the reply.

"A vocal reply? What, no telepathy?" Mark shot the old man a sidelong glance.

"We're inside. I don't need to compete with the wind."

Liz moved behind her boyfriend, fingers now trembling on his shoulder. Mark reached up a slender, strong hand to calm her.

"Speaking of which," he addressed skeptically, "just how the hell did you get inside? I didn't see you follow me, and the window's locked." He suddenly felt Liz's fingers tense.

"Oh my God, Mark. No, I had it open for a few minutes when I got home. I must've left it unlocked."

Mark squinted at the still shadow. "Well. That explains a lot." He pried loose of Liz's grip and ambled forward solemnly. "Now let me explain something to you, Tonto. You can just back your ass down the way you came up." He approached, hoping desperately that this display of all his mustered bravado would convince the stranger to exit the apartment, and his life. "You're scaring my girlfriend and you're making me real damn angry."

The old Native's face became apparent for a moment, illuminated by a brief flash of lightning outside. His eyes were lighter than expected, almost the same silvery-turquoise he wore around his hat. They didn't return Mark's gaze, but peered right through to the frightened woman behind him, and that stirred up all sorts of primal defense responses. But he remained calm, stared back at the ancient man. The skin of the Native's face wasn't wrinkled, more appropriately described as chiseled, worked like cowhide, cracked around thin, reedy lips. He was almost smiling.

Mark found himself closer than he wanted to be, but he summoned up the last of his resolve to drive home the message. "Amscray, chief. Before I remove you myself."

"You don't want to make trouble with me, *bilagáana*..."

The old man grinned maliciously, and Mark suddenly felt the hairs on his neck bristle, smelled the warm, bittersweet stench of darkness and blood and evil waft from the shadows around him. His eyes widened slowly in terror, and he felt hot breath on his neck...

...on the *back* of his neck!

Mark turned only long enough to witness the last vestiges of the transformation. Liz's features melted and flowed away like warm gelatin, gradually becoming scaly, reptilian in substance. Eyes sunk back into the barrel head and glowed bright crimson with lust for fear... blood... carrion. Slender hands became elongated, sinewy digits capped with glistening silver-black claws a foot long. Her smiling mouth opened at the jaw hinges, widened and hissed. Six-inch daggers of dark ivory sprouted from the rancid gums. Mark could see the glint of occasional lightning off slimy strings of saliva, and he inhaled the smell of death.

He fell to the floor, guts heaving. There was another flash of light, followed by a low roar, and Mark knew it wasn't lightning. He rolled onto his knees and looked up.

The old man now stood between him and the succubus, clutching something in his ancient, talon hands. The object seemed to be made of wood, wrapped ornately in ribbons and leather, topped with a stone head, like an axe or a club. A series of feathers wafted from their ties along the handle.

More noticeably, the creature seemed to be wounded. It raised up, brushing it's thick lizard neck against the eight-foot ceiling, and hissed again, this time with a hollow ring of damnation.

"CURSE YOU, LAZARUS!"

"Too late," was the old man's reply. "Happened a long time ago." He struck again with the weapon, and another burst of pure light burned into Mark's vision. The groan was almost pitiful.

"ONE DAY, CURSED LAZARUS, YOU WILL SLEEP IN HELL!"

The old man laughed. "I look forward to the pleasure of your company." He raised the weapon again. "Until then, she-chameleon, you'll have to keep the bed warm."

The creature hoisted a mammoth claw into the air and screamed as it brought the appalling weapon down: suddenly the old man was across the floor, picking himself up like a man thirty years his junior. He'd given it one opening too many, and swore not to let it have another. The thing glared through ember eyes, the crack of a sinister smile evident in the glow from its phosphorescent wounds. It seemed it was enjoying the conflict, thriving on the anger and the fear.

But Old Lazarus knew the ploy. He wasted no time. His attacks were fast and furious, superhuman and lightning-quick, like the pounding of a ceremonial drum.

Mark stared, paralyzed once again by the play of light and shadow before his eyes. He heard the anguished moan of decay as Old Lazarus struck again and again: soon, the demon's ethereal glow flooded the room, streaming impressively from black, leathery scales. He brought the war club down into the skull of the creature, and Mark saw the skin and bone give way, saw the light pour out through its grievous wound. The unearthly blast shone across the room, ran briefly over the ceiling, like a desperate searchlight advertising doom. Its cries were like a Mack truck grinding its gears, plaintive, yet full of anger, strong and malevolent; it cursed them both as the red faded from its gaze and it writhed in agony on the floor.

Finally the old man stood still, heavy with breath and fatigue, weapon at his side. Mark watched as the remains of the creature fell in upon itself, curling and fizzling away to nothingness. The sirens became audible as its light faded away.

Lazarus turned, jaw wet with his own blood. "Check the bedroom."

Mark staggered to his feet, eyes still wide in terror and shock. "Check the bedroom?"

"Come on, *bilagáana*," Lazarus huffed. "Don't have much time."

Mark Crowell shook the fear from his chest and realized what the old man meant. He dashed across the living room, disappearing and appearing through the mottled light that played across the floor. The bedroom door was shut tightly, something Liz never did, and his stomach suddenly filled with a heavy, sinking dread. He burst in, and had only to see the reclining silhouette splayed out across the bed to know they were too late. He moved closer, cautiously, slowly, his mind a thick sponge rapidly soaking up the ambient, permeating horror.

Her throat had been removed, delicately snapped away by the sinister teeth that had almost taken his own throat just moments ago. The sheets boasted a dark stain the same shade as the blood-encrusted laceration. She was naked, her eyes locked open in complete surprise, and Mark knew the ordeal must have inspired an orgasmic glee within the creature that had taken her life.

He marveled at the betrayal she must have felt. Had the creature appeared as him? To take her willingly into her bed—only to become the true horror it was? A delectable death, heightened by the brief psychic surge of absolute, paralyzing terror? Like the boost of a chemical stimulant...or a psionic aphrodisiac?

Anger, fear, denial; a flood of emotional responses hit him with the force of a bullet, and he backed away.

The sirens were closer now, right outside the building. He took a last glance at her mutilated form, noted how strangely, obscenely elegant she looked. And then the desert voice rang out inside his head.

bilagáana. come quickly.

Mark blinked hard and turned toward the living room. The old man was gone. Wind and rain tousled the gauzy curtains and his eyes began to well up with tears.

I don't want to go.

you don't want to stay.

The sirens outside came to a growling halt. Mark rushed to the window. Five floors down, he could see the patrol cars of the Seattle PD with their strobing red and blue, and the officers rushing across the sidewalk into the lobby. The rain had tempered to a hazy drizzle, content only to obscure anyone's vision below. The wind chilled his pale face and he wiped a matted lock of hair from his brow.

Again, the voice came to him.

come on, little hawk. fly away.

"I'm scared," he whimpered aloud.

you want to live, bilagáana, do what I say.

Mark looked across to the neighboring rooftop. Old Lazarus stood atop the building, duster snapping in the wind, war club at his side.

we have much to do, you and I.

The sound of footsteps in the hall made Mark snap his attention toward the apartment door. Voices, mumbling, one heated babble over the others. He looked back at the rooftop. Old Lazarus was gone. Mark Crowell took a deep breath, smelled the salt air coming in off the Sound.

A mad flapping of wings...

He didn't feel his feet leave the window sill.

80

Written in 1991, originally published by Editio Books in 1995. An early stab at short-form horror at a time when I was steeped in writing a trilogy of horror novels (which thankfully were never offered for public consumption), as well as Native American anthropology. The concept of an ancient, indigenous demon-hunter has always appealed to me, and this is kind of a contemporary riff on the succubus legend. The question of what a clearly Navajo medicine warrior was doing in Seattle (domain of the Coast Salish peoples) was really a product of knowing a lot more about the indigenous peoples of the Southwest than those of my then-new city, but the character transcends time and tribe, so I rolled with it.

ESPER

ℬ

An intruder. Someone I know. A company man. We're in terrible danger.

Or is it just another dream?

Gray daylight streamed in through the windows of a sparsely-decorated bedroom in a quiet country home. Sheer curtains hung still, diffusing the light in soft dapples across the quilted comforter. Kyle lay awake, dark hair matted against a square forehead, weathered blue-gray eyes staring at the ceiling. His once-taut, muscled body now softened by the last couple years of early retirement—though a colorful tattoo from a foreign adventure still decorated his upper left arm and shoulder.

This hadn't happened to him in a long time. Not since the Chechnya mission. He chalked it up to general restlessness, and maybe a bit of residual PTSD. After a moment, he turned on his side and glanced at the digital clock on the bedside table.

3:33 p.m.

Valerie busied herself in the spacious kitchen, preparing a late lunch of raw avocado, eaten from the rind with a spoon. An attractive woman in her mid-30s, she wore workout clothes under a zippered wool sweater, brunette hair tied back in a ponytail. Her cello practice complete for the day, her yoga done and treadmill time clocked, she could look forward to a hot shower before heading off to her evening gig with the Seattle Symphony. She half-hoped Kyle would just sleep the rest of the day.

But he thumped down the stairs and shuffled tiredly across the living room floor to arrive at the kitchen bar. It was far too much house for just the two of them, but Kyle wanted to be in the middle of nowhere, and that's precisely where they'd ended up.

Kyle offered a sleepy, "Morning."

Valerie didn't look up. To an outsider's view, this marriage was clearly on shaky ground.

"Afternoon," she corrected.

Kyle reached across the bar, trying to grab the carafe from the coffee maker. Valerie rolled her eyes and shooed him away.

"I'll get it," she huffed.

She poured steaming coffee into a nearby mug, and Kyle tried to explain his bizarre sleep habits of late.

His circadian rhythms were completely out of whack, mostly because of the constant nightmares. He wanted to tell her, but all he could manage was, "Couldn't sleep."

Valerie handed him the coffee, showing a glimmer of sympathy in her emerald eyes. She really *was* worried about him. "You have one of your visions?"

"Yes."

"I wish you'd tell me about it."

"I can't," came the curt reply, which put her emotional walls back up.

"Whatever," Valerie dismissed. "If it works for you."

Kyle uttered a quiet, exhausted sigh. "I've told you why."

Valerie retreated away from him to the other side of the sink, uninterested in whatever excuse was forthcoming. He hadn't been like this when they met two years previous. She hadn't expected it when they'd gotten married last July.

As he sipped from the mug, a quiet hum began in Kyle's head—a hum which became a sharp ringing. It vibrated up the back of his neck and radiated though his skull, deafening him like a severe case of tinnitus. And that's when he glanced down at his right hand.

His index finger was missing, torn away at the second knuckle, a raw, bloody half-digit remaining. Kyle stared at the wound, puzzled. He felt no pain, and could not recall the injury for the life of him.

The doorbell chimed, but the ringing in Kyle's head had drowned out everything else. Valerie looked at him expectantly, since he was the closer of the two to the front door, but by the second ring, it was evident he either didn't hear or didn't care.

"No. No, just stay there," she gestured sarcastically. "I'll get it."

She passed him on her way to the foyer, and he shuffled absently to the other side of the counter to add creamer to the bitter black coffee in the mug.

Valerie opened the front door and had to crane her neck looking up. The visitor was a tall man, ginger hair shaved in a pinfeather buzz to placate a balding pate. Several days growth of beard bristled from his strong jaw, and piercing ice-blue eyes stared at her from deep sockets under a heavy brow. He wore a heavy corduroy work jacket and faded blue jeans, and when he smiled it felt to Valerie as if she were the only woman on the planet.

"Hi there," he said in a smooth baritone. "My name is Richard Landru. I just moved in on the next property..."

Valerie was intrigued. He was rough around the edges, attractive in a rugged sort of way—not her usual thing. "Over at the Jameson place?" she asked. "I thought they were just on vacation."

"Apparently not," Richard smiled. "Mister Jameson was...transferred. For work."

Valerie shrugged, still somewhat dazzled by the tall newcomer at her door. "Huh. Well, Richard—"

"My friends call me Bud."

"Okay... Bud."

The man suddenly produced a plate of baked goods, covered in plastic kitchen wrap, from behind his back. "I brought you some muffins. Homemade."

Valerie glanced at the plate of small, round bran cakes and smiled at Richard in surprise. "I—I was just craving muffins. You must be psychic."

Richard chuckled softly at a joke to which only he was privy. He pushed the plate at Valerie, who took them graciously.

"Well thank you... Bud."

As if to test the limits of his almost soporific effect on Valerie, Richard nodded at the plate. "You should eat them right away, so the nutrients don't break down."

Suddenly Valerie began to see cracks in the shimmering facade of the visitor on her doorstep. Her sense of self-preservation kicked into gear, and she found herself stammering in reply.

"Well, my...*husband* and I were just heading out, but we'll save them for later."

Despite her emphasis on the word "husband", Richard pressed on.

"Just the two of you here, then? No kids?" he asked, peeking past her into the entry hall.

Valerie cooled, dropping her smile completely. "Nope. No kids."

"And what do *you* do...um...?" Richard grilled, indicating she had him at a disadvantage where names were concerned.

Valerie blinked her eyes, flustered and somewhat dizzy. "I'm sorry," she apologized. "Valerie. And my husband is Kyle. He's a travel writer. I'm a musician."

Richard perked up, hoping to hold her attention for just another minute or so. "Oh? What do you play?"

Kyle suddenly looked up from the mug of coffee, an alarm klaxon going off in his brain.

Valerie shook off her daze and retreated halfway behind the door. "I'm...sorry, Bud, but

we got a late start today and we're running behind."

"Absolutely, Valerie," Richard nodded,
stepping away from the door. "I'm sorry to
have disturbed you."

Valerie managed a weak smile. "It's no
problem. And thank you for the muffins."

"Enjoy," said Richard, as he stepped from
the front porch and ambled away toward the
wooded trail that separated the Jameson
property from Kyle and Valerie's.

Kyle was at the door in seconds, almost
colliding with Valerie as she stepped back into
the foyer.

She indicated the wrapped plate as she
handed it to him. "From the new neighbor."

Kyle brushed past her, leaving the plate on
the small table by the front door. He almost
didn't hear her mention she was headed for
the shower. Scanning the leaf-strewn green of
the front yard, Kyle made his way toward the
trail. He'd made it less than fifty meters when
he stopped, more alarms going off in his head.

Valerie disrobed in stages from the bedroom to the master suite bath. Bare feet
padded cold tile as she shrugged out of her
workout top, flinging it on the floor. She
reached into the glass shower enclosure and
cranked the water to maximum heat.

Kyle made a circuit of the property, stopping just short of the woods. He could feel something was off, but he wasn't sure what.

With the temperature perfect, Valerie stepped into the shower, letting the stream of warm water cascade down her lithe body. She gathered her wet hair and slicked it back over her shoulders, her face in the water, oblivious to the shower door sliding open and shut.

Kyle returned to the house, entering through the front door. Scanning the interior of the foyer, into the open living room and adjacent dining room and kitchen, he tried to distill the images in his head. The main floor was quiet and still—just the quiet hiss of water running upstairs in the shower. Breathing slowly, Kyle headed toward the stairs.

Valerie felt the touch of a man's hand on her shoulder and she immediately tensed. "Kyle, what are you doing?" She felt the hand caress her shoulder and gracefully down her arm, while the other hand touched her softly to the left of her navel. "Kyle," she warned, still blind with her face in the shower stream.

When she felt the touch of lips kissing the crook of her neck, she panicked and spun to face the intruder. "Kyle, stop!" Wiping the water from her eyes, she peered through the steam and saw she was alone in the shower stall.

Shutting of the water in a hurry, Valerie grabbed her towel from the hook on the wall, wrapping it around her as she exited the shower.

Then she caught a glimpse of Kyle in the bathroom doorway, and she jumped in surprise. "Goddamnit, Kyle, what are you doing?!"

"Are you alone?" he asked, almost frantic. Too late, he realized how his question could be taken. "I saw... I felt... something."

Incensed, Valerie glowered, pushing past him to get to the bedroom. "Stop fucking around. I have to get dressed."

Chastened, Kyle let her go and retreated downstairs. As he arrived at the landing at the bottom of the stairwell, he turned to the glass door that opened out onto the back deck of the home. The door was unlocked and ajar, a soft breeze blowing through.

Kyle quickly shut the door and locked it, turning his attention back to the main floor of the house. Something wasn't right. In fact, something was very, very wrong, and he couldn't get the pictures in his mind to gel properly.

As he came to the juncture of the kitchen, dining and living rooms, and the entry hall, Kyle turned to make another visual sweep of the interior. And then a tall shape emerged from the hallway half-bath and stepped behind him. There was a dull thud, and Kyle's vision went black.

Silent minutes passed as Valerie dressed for her performance: black leggings and a knit sweater dress. As she sat on the bed, zipping up a pair of knee boots, the bedside lamp flicked and went out. Suspicious, she rose and went to the door.

The hallway was empty, save for a paper towel, soaked through in one spot with dark crimson. It was as if someone was making a specific presentation of a gift. Bending down, she reached out for the edge of the paper towel and gingerly unfolded it—

—recoiling in horror at the sight of a severed finger, pale and still.

She gasped. Valerie knew it was Kyle's. Her mind immediately flooded with the conversation earlier, with the stranger at the door. Not knowing precisely what the danger was, and unprepared even if she did, Valerie strode the length of the hallway and descended the staircase.

She arrived in the living room to find Kyle slouched against the wall, duct tape covering his mouth and wrapped around his hand. He was spattered in blood, his face pale and sweaty. Dried blood caked a wound on the back of his head, and he struggled to breathe. Towering over him was Richard Landru, one blood-stained hand holding a pair of short pruning shears.

He saw Valerie and smiled. "Did you like the gift I left you?"

Valerie's head swam. "What the hell—?"

Richard snapped the clipper together a few times in a mock demonstration. "There's nine more, give or take" he gestured, pointing at Kyle's hands, which the wounded man clutched between his knees.

Valerie staggered dizzily at the stairwell, back to the glass door. "Kyle," she squeaked, "what's happening?"

Richard bent down and tore the duct tape from Kyle's mouth, eliciting a yelp of pain and quickened breath. "Well? Tell her, Kyle. What's happening?"

Kyle blinked, his head resting against the wall. "I saw this," he huffed through painful breaths. "Why couldn't I stop it?"

Richard Landru crouched down next to Kyle, running the pruning clippers down the side of his head. "Because I'm here." Then he stood, angry and irate, pacing the floor like a man wronged. "Kyle, is it now? Making me track you all the way from D.C..." He turned and glared at Kyle with a fury Valerie had never seen from another human being. "Did you really think moving to the other corner of the map would stop me from finding you?"

He straightened, returning his attention to Valerie, who cowered with her back to the glass door, petrified. "Well I did find you. And I'm here. And there's nothing you can do about it." He took a step toward Valerie and she flinched. "And your lovely wife? I'm afraid she's collateral damage."

Kyle watched as Richard stalked Valerie like a feline predator, moving toward her slowly as she stumbled against the door. He was vaguely aware of a familiar buzzing in his head, a fight-or-flight surge of adrenaline. Suddenly he was on his feet, eyes glowing bright with an energy that crackled and burned like static in the air. It was powerful, unfocused, and it swept the room like the beam from a lighthouse, catching all in its path. Valerie held her head, instantly overtaken by a monstrous migraine. A trickle of blood seeped from her nose.

The piercing signal of Kyle's psychic blast continued, rising in pitch and volume. Richard stopped in his tracks, dropping the shears and shaking his head as if sucker-punched. His eyes clamped shut and his hands flew to cradle his throbbing skull, as if to contain his brain matter from escaping. A primal, animal cry of agony erupted from deep within him as a fountain of blood gushed from his nose and ears. A cracking sound within his body echoed into the room, and he went down on one knee, then the other, screaming piteously. His cries of pain were only silenced long enough to vomit more blood onto the floor.

Kyle stepped toward the cowering, screaming man on the floor, eyes aglow. He could feel his physical strength returning—and the control of formidable power within his mind. Whatever interference Richard's presence had been creating was gone; Kyle was back on his game. It was like Chechnya all over again.

Moaning and gasping for breath, Richard collapsed on his shoulder and rolled onto his back, hands quivering in a semblance of defense. His body spasmed with every horrendous cracked bone and ruptured organ. Blood spouted from every orifice as he lay belly-up on the ground, the predator now prey.

Kyle stood over him, memories flooding back. Memories of covert missions in faraway lands, of severed ties with his employer, and of the flight from his former comrades.

They were good. They were very good.

But he was better.

As Richard Landru sputtered for any breath he could muster, an ultimate sort of fear came over his blood-spattered face.

Kyle looked down at him with white-hot burning eyes, and smiled ominously.

"I know how this ends."

ౚ

Original concept drafted in 1999, written in 2014 as the script to an award-winning short film of the same name. I always liked that the narrative just opens on the couple in crisis and includes both a lot of implied history and a very open ending.

Superhero Department Store

&

It had been a bad year for Aquaman.

Popularity had dropped sharply after the cancellation of the *Super Friends*, and things had gotten worse from there. The tabloids were bursting with stories of his being voted Wimpiest Superhero 1988 (gaining the title by default after the death of Robin the Boy Wonder). Article after article followed, detailing his violent confrontation with animal-rights activists at a Greenpeace rally, his ill-fated love affair with Wonder Woman, and his subsequent descent into drug and alcohol addiction.

The truth of the matter was, those whale-lovers had started the argument, he and Wonder Woman were just good friends, and he'd been clean and sober for six months now.

But none of that seemed to matter. He'd gone too far downhill and was too depressed to start the long climb back up the celebrity ladder.

The cashier in Swimwear smiled politely. "I'm sorry, sir," she offered, almost whispering, "your card has been declined."

I watched as the once-great master of the deep hung his head in shame.

"Damn," he said. "The payment must not have cleared yet..."

The cashier nodded. She was nothing if not civil. "I'm truly sorry," she repeated. "If you want, I can hold these for you until you return."

From my position near the rack of SCUBA gear, I was able to see the aging man nod a platinum-blond head and turn away, as the cashier snapped her gum and lowered the desired purchase of Speedos and green dance tights below the counter.

I had to admit I felt sorry for the guy. No one could have known the Sub Mariner would take such a large chunk of his market. But as much as I sympathized with him, I knew not to lend him money. Some heroes were just not good credit risks.

I decided to forsake a new wet suit in favor of browsing the upper floors and made my way casually to the elevator. As I stood waiting, a tall, bald man with sunglasses came up and stood beside me. My eyes glanced at his exquisitely-tailored suit and I found his employee name tag. It read: LUTHOR

"Lex," I said. "I didn't know you worked here."

The man smirked and nodded, not looking at me. "Yes," he admitted. "Menswear."

"Part of your rehabilitation?" I asked.

As the second floor light blinked on, he shook his head. "Just a day job."

"Pay any good?"

Again, he shook his head. "No, but I get an employee discount."

The doors parted and I followed the great-est-but-least-commercially-successful-crimi-nal-mind-in-history into the elevator. He actually seemed to be put out by the fact that the Joker had passed him in the Fortune 500 Arch Villain list three years ago; The Clown Prince of Crime was now in the top five, due more to movie royalties than criminal genius, while poor Lex dangled precariously at number 499—just ahead of Brainiac. *No use whining about it now,* I thought. *Serves him right for choosing Superman as his arch-rival.*

As the doors clamped shut, I noticed two other people in the car with us.

The big guy took up most of the al-ready-limited space with huge feet that must have measured eighteen inches or more in length. The feet connected to legs the size of tree trunks, then expanded upward and outward into a torso that Arnold Schwarzenegger would have killed for...

...or maybe not.

As my eyes raised, I saw the wide, sloping Neanderthal forehead and the tangled mass of jet black hair. For the first time I noticed the color of his skin: a deep, radioactive avocado green.

The lift operator was a young man with mousy brown hair and a quaint red bellboy uniform. He caught my look of recognition and tried to hide in the corner.

"Don't I know you?" I asked, squinting into the shadows.

The young man shook his head. "I don't think so," he said, affecting a low baritone.

"Yes I do," I said.

"No you don't."

"I do. You're Peter Parker, from my Atomic Sciences class at the university." I waved a finger at him and he slowly emerged from the darkness.

"All right," he sighed, "you got me. But please don't tell my Aunt May. She thinks I'm still shooting pictures for the *Daily Bugle*."

"What happened?" I asked.

"Stupid editor fired me. Sure hasn't been the same since J.J."

I nodded sympathetically. "That's too bad."

He shrugged and pressed a couple of buttons on the panel.

Lex Luthor adjusted his tie and cuff links. "Nice day," he commented.

The large green man grunted, and it sounded like a Mack truck throwing a rod. "Hulk not think so."

"Fair enough," Luthor said quickly, and it was then I noticed the unhappy green giant had been standing with his hands crossed in front of his groin. His bright purple trousers had obviously ripped in a very embarrassing spot.

"Third floor," Parker said. "Voodoo Dolls, Jet Packs, Engine Blocks and Anvils."

The doors slid open, and no one made a move to exit. There *was* a large group of ninja waiting to get on, but they took one look at Big-Green-and-Ugly behind us and decided to wait for the next one. The doors shut again, and Parker pressed the button for the next floor. We rode in silence for a few seconds, then felt the car come to a halt.

"Fourth floor," Parker said tiredly. "Menswear, Android Parts, Kryptonite Jewelry..."

"That's my floor," Luthor chimed.

"Hulk's floor, too," The green behemoth rumbled.

The doors slid open and the two departed, Luthor toward a counter stocked with glowing green stones, the Hulk straight to the rack of extra-large torn purple trousers in Menswear.

A statuesque woman entered, arms laden with shopping bags. Her dark hair was shoulder-length and sported a red tint. She wore an extremely tight, shiny black body suit with a silver hip belt and matching bracelets. My mind immediately threw open the giant vault that held every kinky bondage fantasy I'd ever had, and I thrust my hands into my pockets.

"Hello, Natasha," I greeted as the doors shut.

"Hello," she replied politely, melting me with her husky, liquid Russo-Slavic accent. "How are you?"

"Oh, fine," I answered cordially. Some folks called her the Black Widow, and it was no secret that she'd been bed-buddies with the best of them. Regardless of her reputation, I'd been trying to get into her tights for months. Of course, as the rulebook says, the one you want is always involved with someone else, and she hadn't given me the time of day... not that I'd asked.

"So, how's Daredevil?" I inquired with mock concern.

"Oh," she sighed, "he's doing a lot better."

"Has he come out of the isolation tank?"

"Not yet."

"I bet you have to be real quiet around the house..."

Parker squirmed in his stiff uniform. "Fifth floor," he said. "Hardware, Kitchenware, Ladieswear, Sporting Goods, Batware and Lingerie."

"Well," I winked casually at the Husky Russkie next to me, "this is my floor. Maybe I'll see you around sometime."

"Maybe," she smiled, as if it were too much for me to ever hope for.

God I wanted her!

"Say hi to DD for me," I added.

She pursed her lips enticingly. "I will."

I turned to Peter as the doors lurched open. "Give my best to your Aunt May."

"I will, thanks," he replied, briefly saluting, and I stepped out onto the fifth floor. *Hmm,* I thought, my mind clicking away like a pair of wind-up gag dentures. *Kind of funny how you never see Peter Parker and Superman in the same room together...*

I ambled slowly through the first section, which was lined with countless racks of armored bustiers and enormous Wagnerian breastplates. As I passed down the Lingerie aisle, my curiosity got the best of me and I casually snagged a huge brassiere from the rack. As I suspected, the cups were steel-reinforced and sported a series of small hydraulic lifts that functioned as shock-absorbers; kind of a Steady-Cam idea, but for breasts. Sort of *Steady-Breasts*, I reckoned.

I rifled through the rest of the racks and was not surprised to find that the smallest size they carried was a 36 double-D. Everyone knew one of the basic entry requirements for a female superhero was a 36-inch bust line.

I left Lingerie and wandered down the aisle toward Batware. On my way, I noticed a short guy with humongous sideburns and forearms the size of Nebraska haggling with the cashier over the price of a Ginsu knife set.

"I'm sorry, Mr. Logan," stammered the pale youth behind the counter. "I can't come down any further."

"Not half as sorry as yer gonna be, bub."

I sighed, wondering what the world had come to, when a man like Wolverine had to threaten a frightened kid in order to procure a set of claw-replacements.

"I-I can check with my manager," the kid stammered.

"Your choice, bub. Your funeral."

I shook my head, waving as I passed by. "Hey, Logan, give the poor kid a break."

"Shut up," was the curt, much-expected reply, and I entered the Sporting Goods section.

I wound my way past row upon row of *Hobgoblin* jet-powered skateboards and round Vibranium shields painted with red and white rings and finished with a big white star in the middle. I laughed aloud, wondering what kind of fool would carry such a piece of equipment. Talk about a target.

I turned toward the Nautilus machines, and my attention was caught by a big guy in a coal-black jumpsuit. He was certainly impressive-looking, covered from head to toe in guns, grenades and ammo bandoleers. His front was obscured by the various hardware, but I could just make out the shape of a large white skull on his chest. Then I saw him whisper into a walkie-talkie and I was gripped by a sudden fear.

The Punisher was working security.

I hid behind a rack of Thigh Masters and watched as the black-clad vigilante trailed an old lady through Sporting Goods toward Bat-ware. A slender, red-haired beauty stood next to her boyfriend—a tall, good-looking guy with dark hair—as he tried on a pair of ruby-quartz sunglasses. Neither of them noticed as the ancient woman passed by, slipping the boyfriend's wallet into her shopping bag.

There was an ear-shattering *boom* as the old lady exploded into millions of tiny, fragmented bits of spongy red flesh. The smoke cleared, and I watched the Punisher lower the anti-tank rocket-launcher. "Stop," he warned, as the sizzling chunks smoldered and sparked upon the white tile floor.

The Mighty Thor looked up from the brand new hammer he was hefting in his giant hand and approached the Punisher from behind. The assistant in the referee uniform who had been helping the Norse storm god with his purchase made a halfhearted move to remind his client about payment. He thought better of it, and retreated to the stockroom in frustration.

No wonder there's such a high turnover here, I thought, reading the sign that hung over the Sporting Goods cash register: THE CUSTOMER IS ALWAYS RIGHT, ESPECIALLY IF HE IS A NORSE DEITY.

I turned my attention back to the scene at hand as Thor tapped the big security guard on the shoulder. "Ho, knave," he said. "Wherefore didst thou blow apart yon elder woman like so many sunbursts, scattering her bits upon the wind?"

The walking arsenal turned to face a steel breastplate and biceps as wide as he was tall. "She was caught shoplifting," he answered. "What's it to ya?"

Thor merely raised his right arm. "I art verily sorry, mortal. But I have sworn to avenge the wronged, be they small kittens, or old grandmothers who thou doth accosteth with large weapons that spit the great fires of the cosmos..."

"...The hell are you saying?" asked the Punisher, but it was, in the end, a moot question. He was immediately vaporized by a sizzling, crackling lightning bolt from the hammer.

"Young mortal assistant," Thor hailed, turning and gesturing with the large weapon, "I'll take it. Do you accept *AsCard*?"

The coast now somewhat clear, I made my way to Batware, and browsed for a few minutes. I decided on a shiny new Bathook, some Batcuffs and a can of Bathairspray—with no harmful aerosol propellants. I wandered back through Sporting Goods and was joined by a well-built man wearing chrome Bermuda shorts and beach combers. Come to think of it, his entire body was chrome, and he carried a brand new O'Neill cosmic surfboard under his right arm.

"Norrin Radd?" I ventured. "What on Earth are you doing here?"

"Dude," he said, "like I had to buy a new stick."

We walked to the elevator, this Silver Surfer and I. We talked a bit more, and I asked what happened to his old surfboard.

"Dude, I caught this totally cosmic wave an' I was totally thrashin', y'know, an' it was totally killer, but it totally outclassed me, dude, an' I got totally tubed..."

I shook my head, completely unsure of what he had just told me, but unwilling to ask him to repeat it. "Sounds pretty bad," I answered stupidly.

"Dude, it was gnarly."

The elevator doors opened, and we rode back down to the ground floor together. We weren't alone. As it turned out, some mild-mannered reporter who happened to be allergic to glowing green dental floss knelt in the corner and threw up. His girlfriend tapped her foot and complained how much he was embarrassing her. "My gawd, Clark, it's only dental floss! Jeez!"

I tried not to pay attention, and it looked like my silver comrade's mind was on something else completely. "Dude, I'm gonna' head down to the Avengers' Mansion tonight. Wanna come along?"

"I don't know," I said.

"Dude, they're havin' like this party for all the washed-up superheroes, y'know, the unemployed ones."

"Oh yeah?" I asked as the doors opened and we stepped back out into Swimwear. The idea of a washed-up superhero party intrigued me. I would have liked to meet some of the guys I'd followed back in the seventies but whose comics were now worth absolutely nothing. "Who's going to be there?" I inquired as the vomiting reporter made a mad dash for the phone booth outside.

The Silver Surfer passed a rack of neon pink paisley baggies. "Nice pattern," he mumbled.

Short attention span, I thought. *Too many hits from the bong of Cosmic Power.*

"Who's going to be there?" I repeated.

"Dude, like the Human Fly is gonna' be there."

"The Human Fly?" I marveled—no pun intended.

"Yah, dude. And some guy called Stalker."

"Stalker?" I asked in amazement. "The Man With the Stolen Soul?"

"Yah, I think so, dude. And who's that guy with the green tights that used to be in the *Super Friends*? Y'know, the guy who always made the fish do all the work?"

"Aquaman," I offered half-heartedly.

"Yah, dude. Aquaman. He'll be there."

"If he hasn't blown his brains out yet," I remarked. "I just saw him get his credit card declined today."

"Oh, man..." The surfer shook his head. "That is a most *heinous* event. Harsh on the ego, dude."

"You're telling me," I said, approaching the very counter where the transaction had been attempted. The cashier recognized me from before, and smiled as she cracked her gum.

"Will that be cash, check or charge?" she asked all too sweetly.

"Sling it on that, miss." I said, casually flipping my gold *SuperCard* onto the counter.

"Dude, you got a *gold* card? I can't even get a *silver* card!"

I smiled at my chrome companion and suddenly felt very generous. "Oh, miss. Put Aquaman's purchase on my card as well."

And as the young lady rang up my bill, I turned and leaned against the counter, eyes roving nonchalantly about the store. A giant, orange, rocky guy in blue Speedos argued with a man in a green mask and bodysuit with white gloves and a large ring. They seemed to be fighting over the last green kerosene lantern in the Camping Supplies area while a middle-aged professor type in blue pajamas held the object well above their reach with outstretched, rubbery arms. Another guy in a green mask and a Robin Hood hat shot explosive arrows at a hovering figure engulfed in flame. These trans-company disputes could too often be seen in public places; Marvel guys fighting DC guys, DC guys fighting the indies. Green Arrow and Green Lantern had an historical distaste for the Fantastic Four ever since Mr. Fantastic's ego-driven group had swept the Academy of Super Heroes "Capey" awards in March.

I shook my head and laughed aloud.

Through the front doors I could see Wonder Woman shouting at a traffic cop who dutifully wrote out a ticket and hung it in midair next to an expired parking meter. *Some cop,* I thought, *that he can spot an invisible jet illegally parked.*

Moments like these made me glad to be a regular guy.

The cashier handed my card back and stapled the receipt onto the big white paper bag. "Thank you, sir. You have a good day."

"No doubt," said the Silver Surfer.

"Thank you," I replied, and we exited out into the sunny Gotham afternoon.

"Dude," my silver friend began, "so are you gonna go to the party or what?"

I paused, then undid my shopping bag and produced Aquaman's tights and swim trunks. "Give these to Aquaman," I said.

We slapped hands and parted ways, and I listened to the jingle of the purchases in my bag. *No,* I thought. *No party tonight.*

Well, not with the Avengers crowd at least.

I thought of the Batcuffs and smiled devilishly.

And I hurried home to call Natasha.

ℰↄ

Originally written as a competitive speech project in 1983 (took second place in the State Finals), re-written in 1991, published in *Northwest Gamers Network* magazine in 1993—long before the existence of the Marvel Cinematic Universe, before superheroes as a genre were taken seriously by the mass market, and when dumping on Aquaman was a thing. Incidentally, the main character was never intended to be a specific superhero, just someone who lives in their world. However, upon much reflection, I can say with certainty: *of course*, the main character is *totally* Batman.

Second Sight

ॐ

Death does not discriminate. The first thing we learned when we deployed at the Western Front was that the Grim Reaper does not care one jot for a man's skin color—the only hue to which it shows any preference is the dark crimson pumping through his human veins, until the spark of life slips away and that precious red ceases forever.

The Army back home was still a segregated affair, and would be until after the war. So the makeup of the 369th Infantry was "colored", meaning mostly black soldiers with some Puerto Ricans (which we used to joke were there "for some spice"). We'd been given the nickname "The Black Rattlers" by The United States Army, and "Men of Bronze" by the French. The Germans called us "The Harlem Hellfighters", having firsthand experience with our ferocity on the field of battle. Because the US Army wanted little to do with us in a combat capacity, we were loaned out to French command. Our uniforms were American olive drab khaki, but our helmets, rifles and kit were provided by the French.

My unit had already seen action at the Second Battle of the Marne, a shy month of hell. I lost track of my kills after twenty-seven. A particular night raid when we swept a German trench and captured four machine gun emplacements made it pointless to keep a tally of the individual dead. As a reward for our heroism in that campaign, we got sent to the front of the line in the Meuse-Argonne Offensive, and no man would return the same.

We went over the top just before noon on the 26th of September, following a six-hour French artillery barrage, which rendered the land, fortifications, people, and everything in our path the consistency of oatmeal. The first five miles of our advance was through pulverized barbed wire fortifications, where our main enemy was getting stuck in the sundered earth and getting cut on a random shard of metal. We encountered almost no resistance, save for the occasional surrendering prisoners, which we collected and sent back to our lines in small groups. As the sun crested and began its afternoon descent, however, we found the ease of the initial push had been deceptive.

Our objective was the town of Ripont, which lay just beyond a nearly impassible bog. Nonetheless, our spirits were high. Everyone knew the war was nearly over, perhaps especially the Germans. But that only gave them less to lose in the chaos of battle. As Captain Sloane waved us into the muddy bracken, I gripped the Berthier rifle in my calloused hands, checking the slide and making sure there was a round chambered and ready.

Although our French compatriots had shown us how to cut the tails from our wool overcoats so they wouldn't drag in the water and become weighted down, we were going to get far wetter and dirtier than our usual exposure in the trenches. Some of us opted to shed our coats before we entered, rolling them into our packs.

Two dozen men waded into the bog, bayonets fixed. "Slow going" doesn't even begin to describe the agonizing approach to the town. Step after herculean step, mere forward progress felt like wading through molasses. And then, as we came upon a copse of alder trees sprouting from a mound of mushy soil, the gates of hell opened and all the Devil's minions came out to play.

The dappled marshland was suddenly alive with the staccato beat of gunfire and wood splinters. Saplings and men alike were cut in half. Private Coverdale's head opened like a ripe coconut just to my right, spraying me with blood and viscera. Captain Sloane fell into the muck on my left, screaming at everyone to take cover. The Germans had left a machine gun crew as a rear guard to cover their retreat, supported by a sniper aloft in one of the larger trees. I fell to my belly behind a rotting log, trying to gauge where the fire was originating. I knew the wood was too soft to provide lasting cover—this would be a running fight. As much as one could "run" in knee-deep mud and brackish water.

"Desmond!" Captain Sloane shouted at me as bullets whizzed past, "Push forward to Jones' position and see if you can get eyes on that MG!" I glanced down and nodded at the bloodied point of an alder branch protruding from the bulk of his right calf, just above his puttee.

"Yessir!" I replied, nodding at the wound. "You better see to that, Captain."

Then, with a grunt and a splash, I was off. Clutching the Berthier tightly and keeping it above the muck and water, I staggered forward around the log and through the small grove of trees, most of which had been sheared off at about head-height. The sun was hanging red in the afternoon sky, casting long shadows from left to right across the bog. My leg bumped something that felt like a sandbag. Glancing down, I saw a mud-covered hand with a college ring and knew it was Patterson. Half of him, anyway.

Another stream of bullets rocketed from just beyond the riverbank, between the swamp and the bombed-out town that was our battle objective. I hunched over to keep my head low, which made traveling through the mud that much harder. Twenty yards ahead and to the right stood a river boulder anchoring another copse of alder trees. Corporal Jones fired back from behind the big rock, sliding down to a squat to reload a three-round clip from his haversack. His stylish mustache was caked with mud already drying in the afternoon heat.

"Want some company?" I asked, peering through the gap between the rock and the larger of two main alder trunks sprouting from the wet ground.

"Wouldn't say no," Jones quipped, loading the metal clip with wet, trembling fingers.

"Captain wants eyes on the MG," I relayed. "Any thoughts on that?"

Jones nodded. "It's on the bank, just beyond that bunch of fallen trees, yonder." He tilted his head back in a general indicator of direction, and I noted the long wall of raw timber he was describing, about thirty yards away.

"What about the sniper?"

Jones shook his head. "That's another story," he frowned. "But I'm pretty sure he's placed somewhere west of here. Low sun is making it hard to pinpoint." He finished loading the rounds and snapped the bolt forward. "Goddamn Jerries gonna pay for Buzzy."

I glanced to Jones' left and realized Burt "Buzzy" Franklin lay face-down and mostly submerged in the water just north of the boulder. He'd gained the moniker from the clippered fade haircut he adopted on our arrival in France. He was a good soldier, a devil at dice, and a genuine laugh when morale was low. He'd be missed.

Another angry hail of bullets rocketed past our position, tearing through the brush and kicking up steaming splatters of mud. Behind the fallen trees, I could make out a small group of German soldiers trudging through the underbrush, one reaching toward his waist—readying a stick grenade.

Taking aim with my Berthier, I sighted right at his jawline and squeezed the trigger, feeling the comfortable recoil into my shoulder as the shot rang out. The lead soldier dropped out of sight in a mist of red, and moments later, amid panicked shouts, the swamp exploded with mud and body parts. A single boot splashed down to my left, jagged shard of leg bone sticking out the top. From my vantage behind the rock and looking upward, I saw a brief glimmer of light from a tall plane tree behind the soldier, right in front of the afternoon sun. It could have been a trick of the light or a spark of ignited fabric from the soldier's uniform, but it was an equally good bet the sniper was in that tree and the grenade blast had reflected off his scope.

I pulled the bolt back and slapped it forward. Two shots left. For a moment, I considered the F1 grenades I carried in my secondary haversack. I could lob one of the tiny gray pineapples like we used to chuck rocks at crows back on granddaddy's farm. But the tree itself was more than sixty yards distant. Even in my days as a college outfielder that would have been pushing it. No, the math didn't add up. I decided on a different tactic.

I took the blue steel Adrian helmet from my head, pulled a wet tree branch from the muck and inserted it, creating a dummy target. Slowly, I raised the helmet so that the crest just cleared the top left corner of our rock. A crack rang out from the woods and I felt the helmet jerk back and fall off the stick. But I wasn't watching that—my eyes were on the plane tree, about twenty feet up. The muzzle flash had come almost exactly from the location I'd seen the glint in the grenade explosion.

That was my target.

While Jones continued to pop shots at the MG crew, cursing under his breath at the Jerries, I took careful aim at the tree, held my breath, and squeezed the trigger. The Berthier barked, a cry rang out, and something heavy fell, catching in the lower branches.

I reached behind me into the water and grabbed my helmet, checking it over in my left hand. Sure enough, it now carried a tiny depression near the front crest, like a fingerprint in butter. The Adrian helmet was light, and never intended to deflect a direct bullet impact. It was specifically designed to minimize damage from grenade shrapnel and indirect fire. Pulling the strap back over my chin, I flagged Captain Sloane and waved the rest of the unit forward.

Another burst of machine gun fire tore through the wet brush, pulverizing the soggy wood and sending splinters flying every which way. I waited until the gun crew came to the end of the belt, when I would have three to five seconds while they reloaded.

I nudged Jones in the ribs, cocking the slide on my rifle. "Cover me," I said.

Like a well-choreographed dance, I dashed through the stagnant water and mud twenty yards to the wall of fallen trees, while Captain Sloane and the rest of our unit moved up to the rock by Corporal Jones. Now that the sniper was out of the game, I wouldn't have to worry about getting caught in a crossfire and hit from above. And the barking fire from ten more rifles at the rock would make an excellent distraction for what I wanted to do.

My new vantage behind the logs was far better to see the machine gun emplacement. It sat behind a ring of sandbags on the upward slope of a dusty hill about thirty yards to the northeast, the last obstacle between our unit and the village that was our objective. The Maxim gun had a crew of three: a gunner, a spotter and a loader. And it sounded like they were having problems with the reload. I could hear swearing and the clank of metal on metal. The gun had either overheated or jammed. Either way, I'd have to act fast.

Reaching into the bag, I grasped a grenade and pulled it free, extracting the pin with my teeth and releasing it in a high, overhand throw. It came down just short of the gun emplacement. The explosion did little but carve out a chunk of riverbank, shrapnel absorbed by the heavy sandbag barricade. I reached for a second grenade and threw with a bit more force, and this time the effort paid off. The metal pineapple came down right behind the machine gun, and the moment I heard it go off, I sprinted into action, slogging up the embankment like a knight and war horse in one. My lance was a long rifle tipped with two additional feet of bayonet, all force focused behind that sharp point. I saw spasms of motion behind the sandbags, and heard terrified cries and angry oaths, all in German. Within moments, I'd cleared the bog, sprinted up the embankment and leaped over the sandbags, landing with the full weight of my body behind the rifle. The German soldier looked up at me in shock, the bayonet protruding halfway from his rib cage. To his left, the machine gun's back end was chewed to pieces, the gun leaning nose-down over the barricade. The gunner's body lay flipped on its back, a mostly headless corpse. I turned my attention back to the soldier at the end of my pig-sticker and noticed the third crewman was already scampering up the hill toward the village.

Huffing and straining with the effort, I wrenched the rifle away from the soldier skewered on the end, to no avail. The bayonet had penetrated between the ribs and lodged in the spine. It wasn't coming out any time soon.

Almost without thinking, I reached down and pulled the dying soldier's sidearm from its holster, racking back the slide of the broom-handled Mauser and thumbing the safety off. Before I knew it, I'd popped a half-dozen shots into the retreating soldier's back. He collapsed and lay still in a heap.

Then I heard a voice yelling, "Forward!" and I realized it was mine. "MG is kaput! Let's go, boys!"

All was chaos as a rumbling, splashing herd of men came screaming through the marsh, swarming up the hill to where I stood, gasping for breath among the dead machine gun crew.

"Good work, private!" It was Sloane, limping up the hill with his leg bandaged as a small unit of my fellow Rattlers pushed up the last few yards to the outskirts of the village. "I'm putting you in for a commendation—you're a goddamn hero!"

I tossed the pistol aside, not having time to revel in the accomplishment, nor my captain's praise for the deed.

Suddenly a metallic pop erupted near the corner of an old farmhouse at the town's edge, someone yelled, "Gas!" and the men who'd advanced on the town scrambled to put on their filters.

"Mask on, Desmond," Sloane ordered, clapping me on the shoulder. "Let's go take us a town." Then he was gone, and I shrugged out of my pack to more easily access the canvas hood and filter we'd been issued, which hung from a cloth handle around my neck. I hated wearing the thing. It was dank and stuffy and smelled of piss—the common way for soldiers to seal the appliance. But better a whiff of pee than lungs full of phosgene or mustard gas. I struggled to get to hood on, and once properly situated, I realized I had no weapon. I picked up the stock of my rifle which was still stuck in the German soldier. Placing a boot on his chest for leverage, I heaved with all my strength, but his bones held the bayonet firmly and the release was bent. I quickly looked around for another weapon as Sloane ordered the advance on the town and the rest of my unit passed me on the hillside. A Mauser carbine lay on the ground just beyond the gun emplacement, but when I picked it up I found the slide was missing completely. Casting the rifle to the ground in disgust, I turned back to the Berthier and realized there was still one round loaded on the clip inside.

I hefted the stock once again, squeezing the trigger. There was a muffled shot and a spray of blood at point-blank range, and the corpse opened again. The blade retreated as the empty clip was ejected from the bottom of the rifle. It had been enough force to shatter the bones holding onto the bayonet. I quickly pressed another clip into the rifle and slapped the bolt forward, sprinting up the rise to rejoin my unit.

If the Germans knew the war was lost, they sure were acting otherwise. The village of Ripont was wrapped in a swath of what appeared to be mustard gas, like a sickly yellow fog bank creeping across the town square. But there was an additional layer of ghostly white mist just under the yellow, that would occasionally poke through as it undulated beneath. The town looked mostly deserted, except for the German troops occupying every second story with a window into the courtyard. This was going to be a bloodbath, one way or another.

Sloane patted my shoulder again as I approached. "There's our goddamn hero!"

A Chauchat crew arrived and set up at an angle to the first row of houses, opening fire in a straight line across the windows. Any dwellings that still had glass windows didn't after the machine gun tore through. The German rear guard now consisted of a few random infantry left in place as snipers, but the majority of them were put down in the first few salvos from our machine gun. But then the Chauchat locked up with a fatal jam—as they were famous for—and Captain Sloane waved us in. "Let's go, boys!"

Taking up position around the first corner of the farmhouse, I sent some covering fire into the second story of the bakery across the cobbled street as my fellow soldiers moved into the square. I counted down the ammo: *Three, two, one.* Each time I slid the bolt back, releasing the spent shell and racking a new round into place. One by one, enemy soldiers dropped where they stood or fell from the shattered window sills above. I moved from doorway to doorway, snapping off shots as they presented themselves. *Three, two, one.* Each time I chambered a third round, the empty clip ejected below and clattered to the stone street. Despite the knee-deep layer of toxic mist swirling around us, we were picking off the Jerries like low-hanging fruit. We had them on the run. Taking the town wasn't going to be a problem.

I reached into ammo bag and grabbed another clip, pushing it through the open slide as other men continued to fire around me. Despite the conditions, I felt absolutely safe, protected. Then I caught a split-second flash of light from an upper window across the square, and my head snapped back with the force of a bullet glancing off the left eyepiece of my gas mask. The hoods didn't have great visibility to begin with, but now there was a lateral crack across the lower third of the left lens, cutting my field of vision in half and making accuracy next to impossible. Turning back toward the shooter, angry and still in shock, I felt two sharp bursts of pain in my right side and shoulder. The rifle fell from my numb hands, clattering beneath the sea of chemical gas. I staggered back against the flower shop doorway, reaching toward the wounds out of instinct. Another shot rang out, and I felt my throat open at the collarbone.

"Jesus," I mumbled in bewilderment as I sank to my knees in the town square.

Another burst of pain from my left thigh, and a fourth in my abdomen, and darkness began to creep in around my cracked vision.

I fell forward onto my face, knocking the entire left lens free. My eyes seared, flushing wet, and I began to choke as I felt my lungs begin to burn.

Can't breathe.

And I died.

ဆော

My eyes snapped open as I felt myself being supported aloft, gazing down over a stark scene. Two men wearing Rattlers uniforms gripped the handles of a stretcher between them, carrying a soldier's body upon it. I couldn't make out the man in front, but the soldier holding up the back of the stretcher looked like Private Davies, a soft-spoken nineteen-year-old kid from Hell's Kitchen. We'd gone through Basic together. I tried to call out for him, but no sound came out, despite my exhaustive effort. Like a balloon tethered to the stretcher, I was tugged along with the two soldiers and their cargo, this dead Rattler in his tattered uniform, past the field hospital and toward a wagon stacked with corpses. I could only imagine the destination of the wagon.

As they approached the cart, setting the stretcher down ever so gently, a terrible truth washed over me—ice-cold like a Coney Island wave in the Spring. At that moment, I recognized the corpse on the stretcher.

He was me. And these two men were my burial detail.

I felt a strange recoil sensation, as if the invisible tether anchoring me above the man on the stretcher was plucked by an unseen hand. It was abrupt and filled my throat with bile. Suddenly I was pulled downward, and in an instant my lungs filled with air. I could tell I was on my back; the lumps through the canvas stretcher told me it was on the gravel road next to the field hospital. The dead man I'd seen below me was my actual body, and now I was back in it. Everything hurt like hell, and my lungs were on fire. I coughed, one of those earth-shaking coughs that you feel in your spine. Then I threw up everything I'd eaten since the previous night's dinner, and the residue of whatever chemical weapons had seeped into my system during the battle. I could barely manage to croak the word "help" between coughing and heaving my guts onto the road. The most frightening thing was that

I couldn't see. Everything was a murky, desolate void of color.

"Holy moley!" cried Davies. "He's alive!"

"Sweet Jesus!" shouted the other soldier, with an alarm that sounded like he'd seen a ghost at the foot of his bed. The quick footsteps of boots on gravel echoed in my ears. A sudden volley of shouted oaths and orders followed, and I felt the stretcher hoisted off the ground.

I must have passed out then, because the next thing I remembered was waking up with a splitting headache and still no vision. The place smelled of antiseptic soap and alcohol, and the troubled moans of wounded and dying men surrounded me on all sides. I knew I must be in the field hospital.

"Easy, soldier," said a soft voice from the dark. It was warm and feminine, and carried an emotional weight I couldn't begin to imagine. I felt a hand—presumably hers—on mine, turning my wrist to lay a cool finger across it, feeling my pulse. "You're safe now," she said.

I tried to make the words form in my throat, but only hoarse grunts emerged. "N-Nurse..." I sputtered.

"Don't try to talk," she instructed, releasing my arm and reaching up to arrange the pillow under my head. "I'm Dorothy, and you're in my care." She leaned over me, and I got the distinct scent of perfumed dusting powder through the sterile cleaning agents and disinfectants. I knew it was the only scent nurses were allowed to wear in the ward. "There's a bell on the table to your right," she said, placing my hand on the object as she described it. "If you need anything, ring it and I'll be right there."

I reached out instinctively, grasping her arm. With my left hand, I gestured at the bandages wrapped tightly around my eyes and skull. "Wh-What...happened?"

Expecting her to pull away at the sudden contact, I was pleasantly surprised to feel her other hand gently pat mine as I released her arm.

"You were wounded in the push through Ripont," she explained. "Took five slugs and full exposure to a cocktail of gas weapons."

I heard the stool creak as she stood, getting another whiff of dusting powder as she bent, checking my bandages.

"Private Desmond," she said, an almost bewildered note to her voice, "you're very lucky to be alive."

"Th-Thank you," I hissed from my throat.

She patted my arm and stood over the bed. Somehow I knew she was smiling. "Just rest," she said wistfully. "Rest and heal."

Though I didn't know it at the time, the tinge of sadness in her voice was due to the knowledge that I'd never see again. At least, not how normal people see.

ॐ

"Let's see how those peepers are getting on, shall we?"

The doctor's voice was pleasant, smooth as a vintage single-malt scotch. His accent was Mid-Atlantic, the type we'd start hearing on the radio in just a few short years. He was an American colonel, I'd gathered, by the name of Starr, and he always stopped by my bedside for a quick chat while on his morning rounds. Eventually I was able to make more coherent conversation than the hissing croaks the gas had initially reduced me to, and we were able to talk about where we grew up and how surprisingly alike our families were.

I'd spent two weeks in this hospital, literally in the dark, as the dulcet-toned Colonel Starr tended to his patients. Most of us were either French, or Americans under French command, like the Rattlers—who were now becoming better-known by their German nickname: The Harlem Hellfighters. By now, I'd mapped out the entire ward, including the hallways, the WC, and the garden outside the former church that had been converted for its current medical purpose. I'd also formed an impression of every patient, doctor, nurse and orderly in the place, especially nurse Dorothy Brown. Now it was time for the doctor to trim away the bandages from around my eyes and see what was what.

The pressure at my temples, what had been an endless, dull ache, was relieved as the colonel cut away the rolls of gauze around my head and eyes. I could feel layers come away, and yet saw no intrusion of sunlight. Everything was still as dark as it had been for the past two weeks. Finally, I felt the last of the gauze fall away, and the colonel's fingers pry the twin cotton pads from my orbital sockets. I blinked once, twice—nothing but darkness. My thoughts returned to Sunday school, and I remembered a passage from Genesis: And the earth was without form, and void; and darkness was upon the face of the deep.

"What do you see, Private Desmond?" Colonel Starr inquired, his hands gently changing the position of my head as he observed the extent of my damage.

"Nothing," I replied, husky and heavy from deep in my chest. "Not a damn thing."

"Not surprising, really. The damage to the corneas and the optic nerves was extensive."

Something halted in his breath. I could tell he wasn't satisfied. Neither was I, of course. The fact that I wouldn't be the only blind veteran of this war was cold comfort.

Colonel Starr cleared his throat. "There's a specialist in Paris," he began. "I think we'll try to get you in there—"

And at precisely that moment, the lights came on. All of them, all at once. It was as if the noonday sun had dropped right into the ward, white-hot and blinding. Except I was already blind, and this light was searing away the darkness. Every nerve ending in my skull screamed in agony, and I threw my arms across my eyes to stop the pain, stop the light seeping through, to no avail. The pitiful cries of a wounded soldier surrounded my bed, and I realized they were coming from my own throat. I felt hands on my shoulders, both the colonel's and Nurse Brown's. They gently tried to steady me as I rocked back and forth in my bed, unable to escape the light. Let there be light, indeed.

After what seemed like an eternity, but was likely not more than several seconds, the pain receded, and my arms dropped away from my face. My eyes fluttered open, and the light retreated to a normal level in flashes, like shells bursting in a night barrage across No Man's Land. I could see shapes now; shadows and highlights and nuance. It was all a blurry landscape, but there was depth and form. My ravaged eyes washed with tears, and I blinked, washing them with my natural saline. It stung like nettles, or getting lemon juice in a cut. But I let it sting, breathing deeply with damaged lungs as those hands held me.

"How we doing, Desmond?" the colonel asked. "You want something for the pain?"

My head shook no without my conscious input. Apparently I needed clarity for what was to come. "No," I explained. "I'm okay."

The doctor gave some instructions to Nurse Brown, who took a seat beside my bed and continued to monitor my condition. Colonel Starr then disappeared on his regular rounds, promising to return later in the afternoon. I sat up in bed, blinking those lemon juice tears, washing my eyes in stinging agony. After a good twenty minutes, the pain dulled and my vision became clearer and deeper. Shapes, both near and far, were clearly defined. What's more, every shape seemed to radiate with a sort of prism of light. I'd learn later that "halo effects" are common among victims of optical injuries. I'd also come to understand that what I was seeing wasn't a simple halo effect. I glanced to my right, looking into the face of Nurse Dorothy Brown, one of several kind and compassionate medics who had cared for me these past two weeks, but by far my favorite of the bunch. Her face was not more than three feet from mine, and yet gazing at her felt like looking at an unfinished portrait. As much as I'd discovered basic depth and detail in my surroundings, finer features were still a jigsaw puzzle. However, those prismatic rays of light emanated more brightly from her than from the other inanimate objects I'd focused on.

As I glanced around the ward, I noticed every bed had a soldier in it, and every soldier radiated a bright aura of light—like the corona of an eclipse, flickering and flaring in a brilliant dance. Then something in the hallway caught my attention. A soldier seemed to be walking across the hall, but there was no form to his body. The light aura still radiated, but it flared around the outside as if from an invisible silhouette. There was no solid substance to him. Thinking it just another manifestation of my injury, I initially paid it no heed.

For another week, I kept absorbing my surroundings, my vision becoming clearer and more detailed. Colonel Starr's opinion was that everything I was "seeing" was an optical illusion caused by my injured optic nerves sending ghost images to my brain. He couldn't explain how I was able to navigate the ward, the hospital and the grounds, as if I could see perfectly. One theory was that I'd spent enough time effectively "blind" that I'd formed a sort of three-dimensional map of my environment based on my heightened hearing and smell. But when we left the hospital to see his specialist in Paris, and I was still in command of my surroundings, he was officially out of ideas.

It was Friday, the 1st of November. I recall the day was brisk and clear following a week of rain. News was the Central Powers were beaten. The Jerries were on the run, and an armistice was close at hand. A large influx of wounded soldiers had come through the hospital in recent weeks, testament to the final push along the Western Front. French grenadiers, American marines, and even some British Gurkha shock troops from Nepal. Even as I got better discerning faces and details, I never lost the sensation of the "ghost halos". At all hours of the day or night, they'd wander the hallways among the wards. Often, when a soldier died in his bed, I could watch as a "ghost halo" stood from the bed in which the soldier lay, wandering away into the hall or out into the garden. I didn't speak of it to Colonel Starr. When Dorothy came to get me ready for transport, I was already dressed.

"I see someone's excited to get to Paris," she smiled, brilliant shards of light dancing across her head and shoulders.

"Can't wait to see it," I joked.

When we exited the hospital, I found the colonel had requisitioned a staff car for the trip, instead of an ambulance. Nurse Brown and I sat in the backseat, while a young British corporal drove. As we passed along gravel roads, muddy country lanes and hedgerows, we passed columns of the refugees and dispossessed: those made homeless from the ravages of Total War. They were often in the company of Allied soldiers, marching hundreds of German and Austrian prisoners to camps southwest of the Hindenburg Line. I saw the same sparkles of light emanate from every living person, and hundreds more of the phantom halos in their midst.

Paris was alive with high spirits and the same auras of light, and so many phantoms I could not hazard an accurate number. Soldiers home from the front hobbled around on crutches, taxis honked and rattled through the streets, and Parisian ladies laden with parcels wore bright smiles with their Fall fashions.

The visit to the specialist went much as I expected. Read these letters, look into this light, follow my finger. The elderly French ophthalmologist with a well-trimmed beard and crisp, white smock could not determine why I was clearly able to see when all external conditions would indicate I should not. Much to my surprise, Nurse Brown didn't leave it at that. The German gas weapons had affected me—altered me somehow—giving me not only normal sight, but sight beyond. A second sight, she said. Instinct told me she was right.

We stayed the night in Paris, and after that, I knew I would not be going home to New York.

I awoke at 0200 to the sight of two phantom auras in my hotel room. No discernible features, only the absence thereof, radiating a red-tinted halo from a blank outline. Whatever these things were, I knew in my gut they weren't human, and they meant me harm. Without thinking, I leaped from the bed, and found myself hurtling toward the intruders. Whereas most people must obey the laws of physics and land when they jump, I did not fall—I rocketed forward, fists balled into hammers of rage and sheer willpower. Each fist penetrated a silhouette, hands icy on contact. A static discharge as my energy channeled through each of my hands, a brief shriek of agony from either side, and it was over.

I opened my eyes, facing the inside of my hotel room door. Glancing down, I noticed my feet hovered about ten inches off the floor. My hands glowed white and purple, crackling with shards of pure light. Turning to look over my shoulder, I saw my sleeping form still tucked cozily in bed, breathing steadily. I watched the rhythmic inhalation and exhalation for a minute, satisfied that my body would be safe for the time being. Then, turning back to the door, I willed myself forward, and sailed through it.

The hotel corridor I was expecting to be empty was full of phantom halos. They were everywhere. But these specters wandered without apparent purpose, and cleared out of my way as I floated past them. The hallway terminated at a window made of rectangular panes, which I passed through as easily as a draft of air. Knowing I was not in a corporeal body had rid me of any fear of falling or injury, and I sailed gently to the street below, merely focusing my will to make it happen.

A hack drawn by a single horse was pulling away from the curb, and my sudden descent from above sent the poor animal into a panic. Shrieking, it reared and strained at its harness, causing the cabbie to curse and fight with the reins. I gently sailed forward and reached out, making contact with the horse, stroking its neck softly, sending calm intent through my hand. Immediately, the beast settled, and I ascended away as the cabbie came down to check on it. Like a human kite, I sailed over the City of Lights, smelling the myriad scents of food, people, animals, and industry.

I descended into the Jardin des Tuileries, near a slumbering man on a bench. He wore a heavy wool French Army coat, and though his left thigh was tucked under him, I could tell his leg had been amputated below the knee. His aura danced with the same sparks of light that I saw on most living beings, only dimmer and less distinct. I could sense the man's despair, and his morphine addiction, as easily as smelling fresh bread from the oven. By instinct, I reached out, focusing my will through my arms. A crackle of energy buzzed through both of us as I made contact, pushing the sadness away, purging the horror and helplessness—casting light into the dark. The man's body began to shake and tremble, and a trickle of foamy bile spewed from the corner of his mouth. After a few brief, uncomfortable moments, he settled into a deep sleep, breathing normally. The aura around his body surged with new radiance. I was confident that whatever challenges that veteran faced in the future, addiction and shell-shock wouldn't be among them.

My head began to swim, and I knew I'd pushed myself too far in a small amount of time. A few phantom halos in the vicinity began to focus on my location, perhaps sensing weakness. I glanced down at the soldier again, and when I looked up, the phantoms had multiplied. Looking left and right, I could see them springing up from the ground, almost generating out of nowhere before my eyes. Before I knew what was happening, I was surrounded by a horde of faceless phantoms, crowding in from all sides, hungry for the energy I was giving off. For the first time since my apparent death on the cobbled street of Ripont, I felt genuine terror. Terror of my psychic form being torn apart and consumed by these ravenous beings. I realized this fear was keeping my feet anchored to the ground, and that the phantoms must sense fear as weakness. It was weakness that attracted them, much like blood in the water attracts a shark. I had to refocus my will, dig deep within my very soul and produce the strength that would keep the ghosts at bay. One featureless hand reached out and touched my shoulder, and an icy chill struck at my heart. For a moment, I was lost in panic. Oblivion scratched at the door.

But then something remarkable happened.

"Easy, soldier," said a soft voice from the dark.

Clamping my eyes shut, I recalled the dark, featureless landscape of my bandaged vision. I remembered the relative peace and quiet of the hospital ward, and the gentle, soothing hand of Nurse Brown. A sensation of renewed vigor filled the well of my spirit, and I felt my feet leave the ground. I lifted into the air and soared above Paris with eyes still closed, letting the mental picture of my hotel room guide me back to safety.

I found my body still sleeping peacefully in the hotel room. A simple thought was all it took to reunite my astral form with the corporeal one. For the first time since arriving at the front, I didn't dream of artillery barrages or gas attacks. Just quiet stillness.

ℰↄ

I awoke feeling better than I ever had, and made the decision to tell Nurse Brown about my experience over breakfast. After her initial shock wore off, I demonstrated the finer points of astral travel and energy manipulation in the hotel lounge. It was then I discovered I could project my astral form to become visible through the same force of will I employed to soar through the sky, heal a veteran's psychic afflictions, or destroy a phantom intent on evil. Over time, I discovered I could use most of these abilities while still conscious, in my corporeal body. Astonished, Dorothy promised we'd keep in contact after the war. Colonel Starr would likely have some new theories. In the meantime, she and Starr were due to head back to New York, engaged to be married. I jokingly asked what the rush was, fully able to tell from the light emanating from her that she was pregnant.

As expected, the Armistice happened a week and a half later. Like more than a few black American soldiers, I opted to remain in France after being discharged. I began to work with the French government, helping veterans reintegrate to the workforce, helping American military expats like me start a new life "Over There". After months of growing out a curly beard, I started to shave again. I rented a spacious loft in an old building on Rue Chaudron, across the tracks from the cemetery, where I could paint on days when I wasn't doing my government work, and which made a nice base of operations for my nighttime activities. I cut up some motorcycle leathers and found a hooded cloak among the offerings at a theater costume sale. Sometimes I went out in my body, and sometimes I left it at home. I got good enough, precise enough, to be able to knock a thief's astral body out of its corporeal counterpart long enough to allow his victim to get away. When the newspapers began reporting a series of crimes thwarted by a ghostly figure in black, I knew I was on the right path.

Sometime in April 1922, I received a telegram from Colonel Starr, and he came up to the loft to chat. He was working with this consortium of American industrialists, developing a network of adventurers and "gifted" folks like me, to face down a megalomaniac bent on world domination through arcane means. At first, I told him I'd had my fill of tyrants trying to take over the world, but the more I thought about it, the more sense it made that I would use the powerful gift given to me—at one hell of a cost—for the greater good of humanity. Starr left a calling card with the name Colonel Stephen Shaw on it, told me I'd be hearing from him. Apparently Shaw was a higher-up at MI-6 in London, and was putting together a group of gifted people irrevocably changed by the war to help keep the delicate peace in Europe.

By the time Shaw caught up to me, it was May. He arrived at the door to my loft in a trench coat, a wrapped bottle of whiskey under one arm, a valise under the other. He was the archetypal suave English gentleman, with pomade in his prematurely white hair and a patch over his left eye. The man didn't waste time: he had some individual candidates, but needed someone to actually lead the squad the was forming.

"You were awarded a Distinguished Service medal and the *Croix de guerre*," Shaw rattled off in his posh English accent. "And you led your squad across a nearly impenetrable swamp, single-handedly taking out a sniper and a three-man machine gun emplacement. Ripont was taken due to your efforts."

"Just doing what had to be done, Colonel." I could read from his aura's hue that his intent was good. "Who else have you got?"

He opened his leather valise and tossed a stack of file folders on my dining table. "A French vampire, an English robot, and a disfigured Gurkha who fights like a demon."

"Sounds like a motley crew," I remarked, without a hint of irony.

"Some might think it a bit...weird," Shaw replied.

I smirked as I flipped open the first folder. "Colonel," I said, "the moment I stepped off the boat in France, my life's been nothing but weird." As I read over the dossiers, I could tell this bunch would need some coaching, some guidance to whip them into shape as an effective force for good. "What are we calling this unit?"

Shaw pulled up a chair and fished a cigarette from the pack in his inside breast pocket. "We've been working with *The Altered*."

The Altered, I thought. It was an appropriate moniker to describe what the war had done to us. "I can get behind that," I said. "You can count The Seer in."

ॐ

Written in 2019 as the first short story in the second AEGIS Tales retro pulp anthology, which, as of this writing, does not exist.

Dave & Vera

The silver toe of a scaly purple snakeskin cowboy boot pressed down on the gas while the other tapped in time to the rockabilly music on the radio, and Dave let out a deafening "Whooo-eee!".

Route 66 was still the road to run, especially if you drove a red 1963 Cadillac with bull horns mounted on the gleaming chrome bumper, and consciously chose a hot pink western dinner jacket, pleated black and white tweed baggies and an onyx bolo tie as your everyday wardrobe. In fact, with about a quart of pomade in your hair—don't forget the sideburns, man, slick them puppies back!—and half a pack of Marlboros in the breast pocket of your hand-tailored silk shirt, you'd pretty much *be* Dave.

And if you were a slender Barbie doll of a woman who wore low-cut, black sequined dresses, fish nets and four-inch spiked heels, with your dishwater-blond hair piled up on your head and makeup that looked like you'd applied it with a spatula, you'd pretty much be Vera...

...but you'd have to snap your gum and curse a lot.

Vera didn't really spend a lot of time thinking about the fine, gossamer line that separated her from any number of common Santa Fe party girls. She had a john (or in this case, a *dave*), and she screwed him, and he paid her well for her services—though in *his* mind he was cutting her in on their card-hustling profits and not actually paying for the sex in particular, and in *her* mind it didn't make any difference. The money was good, Dave was exciting (if somewhat vulgar, but who the fuck wasn't?), and the hours flexible. So she stayed. She'd stayed for two years so far, her longest relationship by a long shot. She got to see the world—which consisted almost entirely of the American Southwest—she got to wear fancy clothes, she got to eat exotic foods, she got to ride around in a classic cruising machine, sleep in a different town every night, flirt with a wide variety of gentlemen and scumbags alike, and she got to screw Dave (the very concept of which would bring any normal self-respecting floozy to the verge of tears, but which Vera didn't seem to mind at all).

She delicately snapped her gum and cursed. "Shit, Dave. What was that for?"

Dave cracked his sun-baked, roguish smile and glanced over at his painted hussy. They'd just taken some poor vacuum salesman in Winslow for five hundred bucks and Dave was feeling particularly high. "I've got an idea, Vera baby."

Oh God, she thought, *here it comes. Another brilliant Dave-someday-we're-gonna-conquer-the-world-just-you-and-me-baby idea.*

"What's that, sweet-potato?" she asked in mock interest, batting a pair of eyelashes that must have owned private stock in Maybeline.

"I was thinkin'," he began, turning his eyes back to the road as the sizzling asphalt whizzed by under the Caddy's nearly bald tires.

Yeah, yeah, she thought, *you're always thinkin'. Don't strain yourself.*

"I was thinkin' that after another two or three jobs, we could have enough money to actually buy a place."

Vera cocked her eyebrow. "Buy a place?"

"Yeah." Dave looked back at her with a sudden burst of hyper-kinetic urgency. "Like a place of our own. Y'know, put a down payment, maybe get a ranch out near Tuscon or somethin'. Another two or three jobs, we could drive up to Vegas and get hitched, and there you go..."

Vera smiled. Was he even slightly aware of how many times he'd come up with this original idea? Christ, they'd only been together for two years and already she'd heard that speech enough times to mouth the words as he said them. She knew damn well they'd never get that far. He'd been invoking Las Vegas for the past eighteen months, and she knew that they would never go. She had no interest in marrying the guy, had no interest in setting up house with him. She enjoyed their free and rambling lifestyle, with all of the perks, the quirks and the occasional dangerous escape. She was happy with the money, and she was happy with the division of labor.

But, like a good little enabler, she had no interest in striking up discord within such a profitable relationship, and she smiled again, her usual honey-sweet smile. "Why, Dave honey. That's a *wonderful* idea. I'd love to get married and hear the pitter-patter of little Daves and little Veras. Do you think we'll have enough after another three?"

"Well, y'know, maybe four..."

Vera giggled and cracked her gum again. "Sugar-bear, I'd marry you in an instant."

She winked at him, and he believed her.

Just like last time.

If Dave was even subconsciously aware of their little game, he didn't care. He was really feeling good. Five hundred bucks in small bills in his pocket, a beautiful woman in the front seat who wanted to marry him, the sun rising softly over the Painted Desert, and the road beneath the Caddy's spinning wheels. And Flagstaff only fifty miles away.

Life was good.

Suddenly, Vera's voice rang out in a shrill "Holy shit, Dave!" and she grabbed the dashboard, digging in with her bright red nails.

Dave turned back toward the road and slammed down hard on the brakes. What was it? A wreck? A dead body? A coyote? What. The Caddy screeched and fishtailed on bald tires until it finally jerked to a halt in the middle of the vacant road, and Dave squinted out through the dusty windshield to see what had caused Vera to cry out.

A tiny rectangular object sat precisely a hundred yards in front of them, its shiny top glistening in the sun, and Dave thought it resembled a car engine, but it was too small. He gently gunned the accelerator, rolling the car slowly toward the strange item.

And almost at the same instant, they saw what it was, and they cried out in happy unison. *"Beer!"*

The Caddy rolled to a stop just feet from what appeared to be a six-pack of Corona, box and bottles intact and sitting peacefully on the center line of Route 66, fifty miles outside Flagstaff. Dave threw open his door and stepped out onto the slowly-warming concrete, silver toes glittering and shining as he approached the lone sixer.

"It's a six of Corona," he relayed to Vera, who was busy primping in the sun visor vanity mirror. As Dave reached down to pick up the orphaned bottles, he felt an icy chill on his fingers and he smiled. "They're cold," he laughed happily, and when he hefted the six pack into his left hand, he noticed another object about ten feet further down the road. *You're kidding,* he thought. *A bag of limes?*

Limes. This was too cool.

He retrieved the clear plastic produce bag full of the little green citrus and turned back toward the car. "Limes!" he called to Vera, holding up the bag so she could see their great fortune. And as he ambled back to the idling Caddy, he thought, *Wow. Cold beer and a bag of limes. Just two more of the positive aspects of being me right now, I guess.*

Life was even better than it had been a short minute ago.

Dave slid back into the driver's seat and handed his liquid-gold treasure to Vera. She immediately opened the glove compartment and produced Dave's fake Swiss Army knife. Though it probably wouldn't have served him too well had he actually *been* in the Swiss Army, it was more than adequate for opening bottles and slicing limes, and Vera set to work as Dave floored the accelerator and the red Caddy roared back into life. They sped away, and Vera handed Dave a bottle of his own, with a little slice of lime bobbing freely in the foam.

She finished preparing hers, and they clinked their bottles together, grinning ear-to-ear. "To us, Vera baby," Dave proposed.

"Shit yeah," she replied.

And then the light hit them. A consuming, powerful beam of light that saturated the Caddy's interior, flooding their senses with solid white-hot illumination. Dave tried to find the brake, but suddenly found he could no longer feel the floormat. Or the steering wheel. Or the seat.

Then the light was gone, as suddenly as it had arrived.

Dave pursed his lips thoughtfully as he peered out the windshield. "...the hell was that?"

Vera absentmindedly thumbed the pink blob of cinnamon chewing gum wrapped around the neck of her wet beer bottle. "What. What was what?"

"The light."

"The light?"

"The light."

Vera took another swig from the bottle. "Aah, prob'ly just sunlight reflecting on the chrome."

Dave wasn't convinced. "Oh. Yeah. You're probably right." He gently deviated from the road and slowed to a gravelly halt in a vacant truck turn-out.

"What's wrong?" Vera asked.

Dave reached out through the open window and pulled open the door from outside. "Gotta take a piss. Like, real bad."

Vera shrugged. She watched him trot off toward the neighboring ditch, then leaned back and drained the remainder of her bottle. She swallowed the last bit of foam, parted her lips, and negotiated the chewing gum back off the neck of the bottle with one very practiced, pornographic maneuver. The gum was almost solid, but it was her last piece. And she couldn't very well go around smelling of beer.

Dave returned to the driver's seat, a look of absolute consternation plastered on his face.

Vera winked at him. "How'd it come out?"

He didn't smile. "Hurt like a mutherfucker, that's how. You been screwin' around on me, Vera?"

"What? *Me?* Course not." She batted her lashes, noting for the first time a gaping hole in his right cheek that had somehow manifested since he'd gone to relieve his bladder. The wound was dark and swollen, the diameter of a silver dollar, dripping with a yellowish pus and beginning to crust over. She was sure she could see a portion of his cheekbone through it. "Jesus, Dave!"

"What."

"You got a zit comin' in, honey. Bad one."

Dave reached up and angled the rear-view mirror toward his face. He turned the affected portion into the glass, his fingers playing gently over the tender injury. "No shit." He looked again, and suddenly noticed the skin on his fingers had been torn away, leaving only exposed bone, stained with blood. "Man. Got myself a hell of a paper-cut too. Musta happened when we were counting the money last night."

"Musta been," Vera nodded. She reached up to pull down the visor, and let out a horrified gasp when she saw her reflection in the vanity mirror. Her lower lip was missing, sheared away from her formerly beautiful face. Blood coursed from her sundered chin, and bits of white teeth shone through the carnage. "Holy shit!"

Dave revved the Caddy's engine to life, throwing it into gear. "What."

Vera glanced again into the mirror, noting that her left eye was missing, blank black socket staring back in surprise. "This heat is screwin' with my makeup. Look at me. My lip-stick's all smeared, and my mascara's run."

Dave laughed softly as he turned back onto the road. "Don't you worry your pretty little head, Vera-baby. I was just about to find us a motel to freshen up in."

Vera giggled and snapped her gum, blood-ied jaw rotating in the chewing action. "Well good. Can't face my public looking like this."

౸

The motel lobby was completely vacant. Dave strolled to the counter and slapped his hand down twice on the service bell. Dried bits of flesh splintered and fell from his wrist. Vera sidled up behind him as they waited for the proprietor, but no one came.

"Hey!" Dave scanned across the counter, checking the back for any sign of life. "Can we get a room please?"

No response.

"Hey!" His hand came down on the bell again and again, and on the fourth time, his right pinky cracked and dropped completely off. "Hey! Hello?! Anybody home?" He brought up the arm of his pink jacket to wipe across his nose. The nose came with it, landing with a dull thump on the check-in desk.

"Oh, Dave, honey," Vera chimed, reaching into her black sequined handbag. "Don't mess your jacket. Here." She produced a single white linen hanky and held it to the crusty stump where his nose had been. The stained, white-gray foundation of skull was all that remained. "Blow."

The sound was like a tub full of gelatin being sucked through a vacuum hose. She crumpled the hanky and plopped it back into her purse. "Better?" she asked.

"Better. Thanks." Dave turned back toward the counter, his left ear hanging by a thin strap of rotting flesh. "Hey! Who d'ya have to blow to get a room around here?!"

Vera glanced down and noticed her legs looked like she had sat in what she thought was a hot tub, but what had actually been a Cuisinart. Large bands of red and purple striped her legs with open, murky gore. It seeped through the torn fishnets, dripping down into her shoes. She wiggled her left foot back and forth, unconscious of the fact that the heel was broken. "*Tch.* Now I've got a run in my stocking."

"Don't worry, baby. We'll getcha some new ones. We got money." He sighed, and felt his chest sink as the skin dropped into his shirt. Reaching over the desk, he grabbed a key from its hook, noting the almost illegible *118* inscribed on the green plastic oval attached to it. "This is bullshit. We'll pay 'em tomorrow."

Vera cocked her head and heard the cracking of cervical vertebrae. "Good idea. Jeez-us. Place is like a ghost town."

&

Dave located the candy machine three doors down in the cement hallway, inserted his money, turned back to wink at Vera as she disappeared inside to take a shower. He scanned the choices, finally decided on a Mr. Goodbar, and pulled the archaic knob that transformed his stomach's desire into reality.

The candy bar fell with the usual muffled clatter into the metal slot below, and Dave had it unwrapped in three seconds. He began the short trek back to the room, automatically taking an enormous bite of the sweet chocolate. His mouth performed the action of chewing, but the broken hunk of candy fell through the vacant gap in his lower jaw, bounced off his shirt, and plopped to the concrete. He paused, glancing curiously down at it. His almost completely skeletonized hand came up to wipe away another strip of dead skin from his mouth, taking his upper lip with it. Finally, he shrugged and took another bite as he continued back to the room.

*

He found Vera crying on the edge of the bed. Her hair was in clumps, some on the bed, some on the floor, some in her hands. Her back was puckered and white, holes beginning to appear in the dead wrinkles.

"What's wrong, baby?"

"Look at me, Dave!" She stood, angrily waving the stringy clumps of hair and scalp in her hands. There was practically no hair left on her head. What little there was clung tenaciously to small patches of dry skin on her bony skull. "Look at my hair! I can't do a goddamn thing with it!"

"Did you wash it?"

"Of course I washed it! It's just this damn dry air down here!"

Dave scratched his dangling ear, and it fell to the floor. "Shit, baby, we've all had bad hair days. I still think you're one hell of a beautiful woman."

Vera looked at him, tears streaming from her good eye. "You think so, honey?"

"Think so?!" he laughed, moving next to her on the bed and sitting down with a creak of brittle bones. "Baby, I know so! You're just as gorgeous now as the day I met you."

"Aww, Dave honey..."

Dave suddenly realized she'd said something. He turned his remaining ear in her direction. "Huh?"

"I said, why don't we stay in tonight and have some fun?"

Dave grinned (though he didn't have much choice, what with his lips missing and all), and put his arm around her, the fleshy round ball of her shoulder coming off in his hand. He tossed the useless meat to the floor and caressed the exposed joint. "That's a great idea, Vera baby. It's been a while since I been able to make you scream."

"Oh, I'll scream alright," she winked. "Loud enough to wake the dead."

∽

"That's a bunch o' bullshit," Sharon drawled, waving a dismissing hand. The silver shell of the vintage Airstream trailer shone brightly in the thin orange light from the stone fire pit. She raised the Corona to her lips, thought about it for a split-second, then lowered it back to her lap.

Pete leaned back in the aluminum lawn chair and smiled. Sharon's movements were not lost on him. Kenneth simply sat bug-eyed, completely enthralled, and Pete knew he'd told it well. He raised his own beer to the darkening gunmetal desert sky, smiling his round, baby-faced smile. The evening wind tousled his gray hair. "I shit you not. Ladies and gentlemen, to Dave & Vera."

Sharon sneered, weather-beaten, thin lips curling under a middle-aged hawkish nose. "Bullshit."

Kenneth shivered. His wrinkled eyes had seen a lot of the world, and yet remained childlike and innocent. He was scared shitless. "Sharon, girl, don't mock the dead." He turned back to Pete, brow furrowed into a mask of fear. "They *were* dead, weren't they?"

Pete laughed aloud. "I call them the *unquiet* dead."

Sharon huffed, still unbelieving. "Fine. Fine. *Unquiet* dead then." She looked twice at the bottle in her hand before she drank from it again.

Then Pete caught a glimpse of headlights on the desert road, and his lips raised into a knowing smile. "Speak of the devil..."

Sharon and Kenneth stood from their chairs and whirled to face the highway. Pete raised his bottle again, toasting the approaching vehicle.

There was a waving of skeletal hands in the moonlight, and a strong double-honk from the horn as the red Caddy sped by.

⁊⁊

Written in 1992 as a way to merge my love of rockabilly culture with some dark comedy, gross horror and a "Tall Tales of the Old West" kind of vibe. It's completely bizarre and I still love it.

Calico Kids

∞

The digital clock in the Soundesign cassette deck blinked over to 7:30 a.m., and Blue Öyster Cult's "Burnin' For You" erupted from the tiny pair of speakers under the faux wood case. A soft breeze blew in off the river, bidding the decades-old flower-print curtains dance to the song, carrying the competing odors of pulp mill and salmon cannery to the nostrils of the slumbering teenage boy.

A.J. stirred at the sudden assault of smells and power chords, and reached for his glasses on the milk crate nightstand. Contorting into a semi-reclining position, he grabbed the clock and turned it toward him, yawning.

Home in the valley
Home in the city
Home isn't pretty
Ain't no home for me

Alan Jennings was small for his age—thirteen among peers who were already fourteen and dating. What his dad called "shit-brown" eyes squinted through an unruly mop of dishwater blond hair, the bangs kept long to hide the acne on his forehead. His left cheek was already pitted from a fishing accident when he was eight, the hook still somewhere in his tackle box.

Had he really set his alarm for 7:30? Sure, the extra half hour of sleep was badly needed after studying into the wee hours, but... 7:30? Was he insane?

A.J. was a good student. He was also short, skinny, far-sighted, and thus a target for harassment of every type imaginable. Being a font of local history and at least three or four juicy conspiracy theories didn't help matters. But he was scrappy, and fast, and used humor as a finely-honed weapon. Or at least he used to, before he got on Liam's good side. This year had actually been bearable due to the bully's protection. Seventh grade last year had been a living hell.

Home in the darkness
Home on the highway
Home isn't my way
Home will never be

A.J. jumped from his bed and pulled a three-day-old pair of Levi's over scrawny, pale legs. It was Friday of finals week, with just eight days left in the school year. For A.J., that meant graduation from Calico Junior High ("Go Herons!") and entering as a freshman at Calico High ("Go Lumberjacks!"). He shrugged into a *Star Wars* logo tee and a red flannel shirt with a selection of mechanical pencils in the pocket. His socks were the only article of clothing clean from the drawer.

Burn out the day

Burn out the night

I can't see no reason to put up a fight

He hopped out of his bedroom and down the hall as he tried to wrestle his feet into a pair of leather Nikes from last year. The shoes barely fit, but he knew he could look forward to some school clothes money from Gram this summer. The small Craftsman bungalow on Ash Street was quiet and empty, Mom and Dad having left for work at least thirty minutes ago.

I'm living for giving the devil his due

And I'm burning, I'm burning, I'm burning for you

Plucking a foil pack of two Pop Tarts from the box on the kitchen table, A.J. grabbed his jacket and backpack from the corner behind the door and ran into the wide world outside. Still groggy from the late night cram session, he pulled his Huffy Thunder Road BMX bike from the side of the wood pile under the eaves of the carport and saddled up in a single, well-practiced motion. Letting gravity give him an extra burst of speed down the hill, A.J. lowered his head into the late spring breeze and sped toward the road to school.

He had an algebra test in first period, and he was late.

Calico, Oregon was a small, blue collar community of 7,000 rugged individuals, nestled on the north bank of the Rogue River, less than five miles due east of Gold Beach. Originally a mining boomtown in the 1850s (named for colorful silver prospector "Calico" Jim Broughton), a mining accident in 1882 had made the old site unlivable, forcing the residents to move a couple miles down river.

A.J. dropped down from Hill Avenue onto the bottom half of Hillcrest Drive, which became Lamont Street as it intersected with 4th Avenue. His route was so etched in his brain that he could ride it blindfolded, as long as there wasn't any other traffic. South on Lamont, left on Pioneer, where vibrant banners lining the street reminded residents of the upcoming town centennial in August. Then a right onto Silver Street, which ran alongside the school's athletic field.

He knew a fair amount of local history, how Calico had reinvented itself as a respectable logging community after the re-charter. The access road he now used as a short-cut to school hadn't seen a truck in over a decade; most deliveries to the pulp mill usually arrived on the river frontage road. The pulp mill had been the primary employer here since 1920, followed by the fish cannery on the west side of town. Most other businesses—from the diners to the real estate office, the bars to the auto garage on Third Avenue—supported the mill and cannery workers and their families. They also employed wives and teenagers.

A.J. approached Calico Junior High at high speed and found Kristof Korolewski already locking his bike to one of the stalls out front. Kris was 14 and a first-generation American, his Polish family having immigrated to the States after World War Two. He was blond and apple-cheeked, and a good half-foot taller than A.J. The Korolewskis owned and operated the Silver City Diner on Second and Durham, complete with a small "arcade"—which was really just an old coat check room crammed with *Space Invaders, Asteroids, Pac-Man*, an old *Sportsman* duck hunting game, and a couple pinball machines. The diner even featured an old grandmother who spoke no English and had a milky eye, but who made the most amazing pirogies you ever tasted. Kris worked dinner shift, and was never without a ready supply of those very pirogies. He tended to use them to buy the friendships in his life, which was really unnecessary. He was a nice kid to begin with.

"Hey Kris," A.J. hailed as he skidded to a halt and dismounted the banana seat like a cowboy in an old western. He pulled the front wheel into the rack space next to Kris and undid the combination lock without even looking at it. He could see their friend Liam's "Frankenbike" opposite their own cycles, a patchwork of primer-gray aluminum, cannibalized black BMX parts and a seat held together with duct tape.

"You're late," Kris joked, knowing full well they were in the same algebra class, and would share the same fate for being tardy.

A.J. glanced down at "the Kricyle"—an old Schwinn cruiser with knobby tires, advertising placard in the center frame, and a milk crate basket at each end for delivering take-out to the local community. "Up late too?"

"No doubt," Kris answered, adjusting the strap of his backpack on his left shoulder. "Gotta ace this final or hello, summer school."

"Your folks wouldn't do that to you," A.J. dismissed with a wave. "They need you at the diner."

The two boys left the long rack of Huffy street bikes, Schwinn BMX conversions, and

Raleigh Choppers, heading toward homeroom and their math final.

"Besides," A.J. said as he playfully slugged his larger friend in the shoulder, "you've got this."

&

It was lunchtime by the time news had filtered over from the high school: Jeannie Wells hadn't shown up for school, and hadn't come home last night. Ordinarily, gossip of this kind would have slipped past them. The high school sophomore was popular, full of school spirit, and considered attractive by her peers —all things A.J.'s gang weren't. However Calico was a small American town, and as with most small American towns, connections ran like a nervous system beneath the surface.

Jeannie's parents had been close with A.J.'s—so close that they'd been asked to be his godparents. Three years ago, a brain aneurysm had claimed Sally Wells, leaving David Wells to soldier on alone, raising his teenage daughter and splitting his time between the paper mill and Elliott's bar two blocks away. A.J.'s family hardly saw David Wells anymore. And Jeannie had withdrawn into her very specific social circle, sighted less frequently than Sasquatch by A.J. and his ilk.

Despite her tragic family situation, Jeannie was known as a good girl and a straight-A student, so it was highly newsworthy that she hadn't returned the previous night.

Liam approached the outdoor picnic table and A.J. braced for a noogie that never came. He would have taken it, gladly, just to be reminded of what he was avoiding by being under the protection of William "Liam" Scott. Hidden beneath a camo Army jacket three sizes too big, Liam was six feet and 150 pounds of the kind of coiled muscle only seen on skinny, under-nourished kids who lifted weights. The 14 year old hadn't picked up the shaving habit yet, either, so scraggly black hairs poked randomly from his mouth and chin. An uncombed mass of curly, dark hair fell forward over a pair of mirrored aviators, which hid ever-wary chestnut eyes. His ruddy complexion spoke of Shasta and Coquille ancestry somewhere back, a notion he was the first to reaffirm with tales of his mother's alcoholism, mostly so no one else could bring it up first.

But today was not to be about drunk mother stories. Today was all about Jeannie's disappearance.

"You hear about Jeannie?" Liam asked.

Kris joined them, producing a paper lunch sack from his backpack. "In gym, they were talking about finding her body in the creek out by Old Town."

A.J. rolled his eyes. "Bullshit. The rumors are getting out of hand."

"What do you think happened?" Kris threw a quizzical glance at Liam, opening a smaller paper bag full of pirogies and offering them to the erstwhile bully.

Liam took a handful of small Polish pastries and ate them one by one as he pondered. "You know Jeannie's dating Eric Somerville..."

"Yeah," Kris nodded, "they're always hanging out at the diner."

A.J. squinted. "Were they there last night?"

"Sure. They each had a Coke and shared a basket of fries—"

"I wasn't asking what they ordered," A.J. sighed.

Liam grabbed A.J.'s can of Rondo and took a swig. "They probably went up to The Bluff to park."

Kris and A.J. exchanged a look that was somewhere between jealousy and bewilderment. Neither had been on a date, much less "parked"—that was an activity reserved for high school kids—but both were a little curious, and growing more curious by the month. Indian Bluff was a well-known spot favored by teens with access to four-wheeled vehicles and later curfews. It was a turnout on an old logging spur from North Bank Rogue River Road, overlooking the site of Old Calico and the adjacent clearcut. Although "The Bluff" was shielded by forest to the west, sunsets bathed the ghost town in beautiful hues of pink and orange, almost an incentive to stop making out for five minutes and bask in nature's glory.

"How do you know?" Kris asked.

Liam shrugged. "I don't. Not for sure. But ever since Eric got that Nova running, they've been going up there a lot."

"We should look for them," A.J. blurted. It was more forceful than he'd intended.

Liam raised his eyebrows behind the glasses and chuckled. "Okay, hotshot. Just how do you figure we go about this?"

"We should go by Jeannie's house first," A.J. replied. "Check on Mr. Wells. He works the swing shift at the mill, so he might still be home when we get there."

"If we meet at the diner," Kris added, "I can have Baba make some fresh pirogies to take over."

Their plan was foolproof. The three boys had all arranged to take a 7th period prep this semester. Kris actually had a legitimate reason, as he worked after school at the diner, but Liam and A.J. followed suit, and on days when Liam wasn't in detention, it meant an early start on activities like playing *Dungeons & Dragons* at A.J.'s, fishing at their secret spot up the river, or besting one another's high score on Pac-Man at the diner.

After a quick stop to pick up Kris and a fresh bag of pirogies, they saddled up and pedaled to the outskirts of town, where a small manufactured home sat on a shy acre of wooded land. A.J. had been here many times prior to the death of Mrs. Wells, not so much in the past couple years.

Mr. Wells' red Chevy pickup was nowhere to be seen.

The three boys shared a conspiratorial look, and without a word, walked their bikes around to the back door, which had been left unlocked—as Liam immediately found by testing the handle.

"Nobody's home, guys," Kris observed.

"Yeah, no shit, Sherlock," Liam scowled. "We're just gonna see if there are any clues to where Jeannie might be, leave the pirogies and a note."

A.J. shivered but refused to show his nerves. "What are you worried about?" he asked, following Liam inside.

"Aside from prosecution for B&E, nothing," Kris retorted, looking at the greasy bag of food in his left hand before taking a deep breath and following the other two boys.

The home was dim from the aluminum blinds covering the windows and turned closed. The avocado shag carpet held the smell of cigarettes and winter mildew. A.J. thought the place could use some airing out.

While Kris took a lookout position at the kitchen bar, setting the bag on a counter of mottled yellow Formica, Liam and A.J. crept quietly down the hall to the bedrooms. Mr. Wells' door was open and revealed a dark, disheveled room beyond: the bedclothes were a jumbled mass, mingled with the laundry pile, and empty beer bottles littered the night-stands and floor. It smelled like the family room where they'd entered the house, with the addition of adult male body odor. Wells worked a physical job, so it was to be expected that his bedroom would harbor that scent.

Jeannie's bedroom door was closed, but none of the interior doors—save the single bathroom—had locks. For whatever reason, A.J. felt a sort of protective instinct for the Wells family, and he muscled past Liam to be the first into the room.

"Easy, cowboy!" Liam chided.

A.J. ignored him. The room stood in complete contrast to the rest of the home, bright and airy and colorful to her dad's dark lair. Mall posters of Duran Duran and Rick Springfield lined the walls next to a concert print of

Quarterflash. Magazine photos of Pat Benatar and The Runaways were thumbtacked to the cheap drywall over Jeannie's vanity. A single black and white 4"x6" portrait shot of Eric Somerville was tacked over the other pictures, staring distantly at the photographer.

Liam went to the far side of Jeannie's wrought-iron bed and carefully looked through the sundry "girl" things littering her study desk. "She must have a journal or something—"

"No way, man," A.J. shot back immediately. "We're not snooping in her..." The last words were interrupted as he absently nudged open the nightstand drawer, revealing a locked pink diary. "Shit."

Suddenly Kris called from the kitchen. "Uh, guys?"

The pickup's tires on the gravel drive were already audible, and A.J. bolted from the bedroom. Liam followed, pausing long enough to grab the diary from its drawer and close the bedroom door behind him. He pocketed the pink book in his Army coat and made the back door just as Kris exited.

By the time Mr. Wells had parked the truck and come to the front door, the boys and their bikes had disappeared into the trees.

They skidded to a sideways halt in a forest clearing just north of town, above a small deer path that led down to the main road. The burned-out stumps of old-growth cedar created semi-sheltered structures the local teens used for camp outs and picnics, or cutting class to pound beers and smoke weed. Liam produced Jeannie's diary from his pocket, and A.J.'s eyes widened in utter disbelief.

"What the hell—??"

He was silenced by the appearance of the Swiss Army knife in Liam's other hand. A.J. wasn't so much surprised—Liam was precisely the kind of kid who packed a Swiss Army knife, and other sundry tools and weapons, in various pockets on his person. He was more apprehensive at how the bigger kid, the bully of bullies, intended to use it.

He set the diary on his bike seat, flipped the small blade open and fished the toothpick from the utility knife's red metal housing, and within a minute had picked the tiny lock holding the book closed.

A.J. and Kris closed around Liam slowly, their curiosity trumping their nervousness.

To his credit, Liam opened the diary at the end and scanned backward, clearly looking only for clues to Jeannie's possible whereabouts. A.J. felt a familiar sense of proprietary jealousy as Liam flipped the pages back one by one.

"Come on, man," he scowled, kicking a foot into the dusty floor of the clearing. "What does it say?"

Liam flipped another page, working his way backward in time. "Well, her home life is more fucked up than we thought. Pop's drinking himself to death, and she's having trouble dealing with her straight-A, squeaky-clean image."

Kris stared at Liam like he would a riveting TV show. A.J. just frowned and dug his hands into his hoodie's kangaroo pocket. "Shit."

"She knows Eric's planning on leaving after he graduates... seems torn between wanting to take off with him and staying here to help her dad."

Liam did his best to keep his report clinical and avoid any salacious interpretation of Jeannie's innermost feelings poured out on paper. "As I thought. They were parking at the Bluff. Like, a lot."

"Close it up," A.J. ordered. "Let's go to the Bluff."

"What else?" Kris asked innocently.

A.J. wasn't having the delay. "What do you mean, 'what else'? They went to the Bluff to park. Close it up! We should be looking for clues there!"

"I think he means, 'what else did they do up there?'," Liam winked at Kris. "You did take sex ed, right?"

"Come on guys!" A.J. went back to his bike and threw his leg over the frame to straddle it.

Kris blinked. A filmy sweat broke out on his forehead.

Liam leaned over to him, lowering his voice to a near whisper. "They've been doing the dirty," he said, making a circle with the fingers of his left hand and penetrating it repeatedly with his right index finger.

A.J. pretended not to hear, pedaling out of the clearing in a huff. Liam replaced the knife and the diary in their respective pockets and picked up the Frankenbike from the ground. He was away almost immediately. Kris ran to his bike and followed Liam out of the clearing, trying to lose the red flush from his nose and cheeks.

સ૦

It was a short half-mile to North Bank road, then the better part of a ten-minute ride east along the river to Indian Bluff. As they approached the turnout, their presence was noticed by Deputy Pete Halverson, his thick face with close-set brown eyes glowering from beneath the brim of his flat-brimmed "Smokey

Bear" hat. Halverson was just 28, but he'd grown up in Calico, been a high school football star, was injured in a game, and never left town. Although the county seat was five miles away in Gold Beach, Pete still lived in the family home in Calico. He'd opted to remain a big fish in a small pond instead of exercising an ounce of ambition.

Halverson's brown patrol Bronco was parked at an angle on the bluff, nose pointing across the clearcut toward Old Town. The emergency light bar atop the vehicle flashed red and blue, though the engine was shut off, and the Curry County insignia shone in stark contrast to the white door panel. The deputy stepped forward and held up a hand, signaling the boys to halt.

As A.J. braked to a stop on the turnout, he noticed Halverson was standing next to a strange marking on the ground. Kris pulled up next to him and noticed it too—the shape looked like it had been burned into the very rock at their feet. It appeared to be a triangular glyph four feet across, with a circular point in the middle, and sections of each side cut away so that only the corners were visible. A.J. immediately thought of the town scare back in 1972, blamed on a Satanic cult that supposedly lived in the Rogue River-Siskiyou National Forest. Two teens had disappeared from the Bluff and never returned. Some folks thought they'd just left town. Others, like A.J., remained convinced it was the cult, and that they were still out there in the deep woods of Oregon, sacrificing babies and eating s'mores with the Dark Lord.

Liam slowed and hung at the back of the group.

"Hold up! Hold up!" Halverson ordered with a level of official bluster that would have been hilarious if it weren't so sad.

"What's... uh, what's going on, Deputy Halverson?" A.J. inquired.

"Hey, Pete," quipped Liam from the back of the group. The subtle disrespect of a tin badge had the desired effect of a glare from Halverson.

"Jennings," Halverson pointed at A.J., "you're tight with the Wells family. Any idea where Jeannie or her boyfriend might have gone?"

A.J. swallowed hard. "Uh, no... I don't actually... I'm not that close..."

"Pete? Who's up there?" cried a voice from below the lip of the bluff. The three boys pushed their bikes forward, still astride, peering over the edge of the turnout. The road's edge was without a guard rail, and fell away a good fifty feet to the floor of the clearcut below. Sitting nose-down at the bottom of the steep grade was Eric Somerville's 1974 Chevy

Nova, midnight green save for splotches of primer gray. The windows were up, doors locked, emergency brake set. The car was undamaged, which was a head-scratcher, given it looked like it had gone off the bluff and slid down the hill.

Standing next to the Nova, just paces away from her own Bronco with flashing lights, was Sheriff Linda Chavez. She was what folks called "compact". A solid 150 pounds of muscle in a petite 5'2" frame, Chavez looked like she could take Halverson in an arm-wrestling match, and probably had. Her shoulder-length, raven curls were pulled back in a low bun under her hat, and her shirt cuffs were rolled up to her elbows, exposing well-tanned arms—unusual in a region of pale people who liked to joke, "Oregonians don't tan, they rust." She was proud of her Latina ethnicity and of being the first woman to hold the elected post, after the previous Sheriff of Curry County was forced to resign amid numerous sex abuse scandals and a rather large wrongful death lawsuit. "What are you kids doing out here?"

A.J. liked Sheriff Chavez. He waved slightly and managed a smile. "Hi Sheriff. We were, um, just riding. Kris found a fishing spot up by Lobster Creek Bridge." He immediately regretted the statement, as the three carried precisely zero fishing equipment, and he was sure Deputy Halverson would take notice of that.

To everyone's surprise, Pete kept his attention on the glyph, snapping a shot with a Polaroid camera and placing it on the Bronco's hood to develop.

Chavez squinted from below the group of boys in the turnout. "You're not headed into Old Town, are you?"

"What? Um, no. It's off limits." A.J. answered dutifully.

"Correct," replied the Sheriff. "Don't forget that. Alright, *vámonos*."

Halverson began waving them away immediately. "Let's go. Clear out, boys."

Chavez returned to her investigation of the Nova, and the three teens returned to the main road.

They rode on, equal parts shaken and exhilarated by the encounter with Curry County's finest. Kris pedaled hard to center himself in the pack.

"Did you see that... what was it? A shape, I guess?"

A.J. nodded. "It seemed familiar to me."

Liam was more sanguine. "This is worse than I thought," he scowled. "Eric loves that car. There's no way he would have just left it there. And did you notice the damage?"

"What damage?" Kris frowned, trying to re-member.

"Exactly," Liam said. "There wasn't any. How does a Super Sport with the weight of a 350 V-8 under the hood roll down a fifty-foot grade and just stop? It should've rolled out into the clearcut at least. But I didn't even see a ding on that front-end."

"Parking brake?" A.J. mused.

Liam shook his head, standing up on his pedals to coast. "I'm not buying it. The whole thing smells like pee."

"So whether they left or were taken by force," Kris began thoughtfully, "where is the most likely place to go?"

"To hide," Liam asked, "or to be hidden?"

"Either one."

A.J. stood and pumped his pedals. "Old Town," he said, angling east onto the old dirt access road.

Kris and Liam followed, pedaling silently for the remainder of the journey, pulling off the main road and onto an old dirt path made by wooden wagons a century ago.

As the calendar neared summer, southern Oregon had the virtue of much later sunsets, the afternoons and evenings seemed suspend-ed in an endless golden stasis. A.J. knew they wouldn't completely lose light until 8:49 p.m., and he had until then to check in with his parents. That left them with a solid couple hours to search before even considering the trip back. The boys rode with purpose, the only sound the rotation of greased bicycle chains driving gear sprockets and the occasional thump of a lose rock kicked aside by a knobby front tire. With the late sun at their backs, they turned with the wheel ruts to make their final approach from the south.

Old Town Calico resembled an abandoned western movie set, down to the scrub brush poking up from packed, dry dirt, and old buildings on the verge of collapse. It had been a typical boomtown with a single main street, on either side of which had stood a line of timber frame buildings. All the necessities of Old West life had once been here: the hotel, saloon, sheriff's office, and livery, with the bank strategically placed at the north end of the strip near the mine entrance. Once proud facades sagged, weathered and rotten, with many of the buildings having collapsed or been damaged by the sinkholes that accompanied the mine explosions and toxic gas cloud that followed.

Liam was first off his bike, ditching the monstrosity behind an old wooden outhouse that remained mostly upright at the southeast corner of the main street. The small structure had been a satellite of the saloon, which stood deceptively intact just a few yards to the north. Wielding his treasured Maglite 6-D like a weapon, he approached the sagging door of the outhouse.

"Lucy, I'm home!" he chirped, hooking the door with the toe of his Army boot and flinging it open.

He disappeared inside as A.J. and Kris dumped their bikes next to Liam's, taking stock of their surroundings. Several of the more precarious buildings—including the saloon nearby—were adorned with warning placards from the Curry County Sheriff's Department, advertising how unsafe the location was and what the legal consequences of trespassing were. Not that Curry County actually had the manpower to enforce such warnings, which was why exploring Old Town was a rite of passage.

Kris and A.J. stepped out into the street, sun low on their left. Liam had just emerged triumphantly from the outhouse with a century-old horseshoe nail when they heard it: a faint feminine cry for help.

Each boy shivered in succession as they ran through the possible sources for such a sound, finally returning to reality. The cry was of human origin, and it was coming from inside the saloon.

Liam pocketed the nail and turned his flashlight toward the saloon doorway. The swinging doors had fallen off long ago, and the doorway itself was skewed at a precarious angle like a funhouse ride. The three boys entered the darkened, dusty interior. Tables and chairs had been left in place, now broken and scattered around the outer orbit of the establishment. The bar itself had broken in the middle, caved into a V shape, the long horizontal mirror behind it shattered and mildew-spotted. The center of the saloon floor had collapsed into one of the many sinkholes that ate Old Town, broken planks of oak thrust upward in a conical spiral.

The beam from Liam's Maglite roamed across the sundered floorboards, down into the pit that fell almost ten feet below. As it hit the pale shape of a human hand, the same cry wafted up from the pit in the floor, and A.J. knew they'd found her.

Jeannie Wells, barefoot and clad in torn blue jeans and a zippered hoodie, lay at the bottom of the saloon sinkhole. Her face was ashen and her hair stringy and matted with sweat. A.J. noted the same glyph from Indian Bluff seemed to be tattooed—or rather, *branded*—into the flesh of her inner right wrist.

"Help, please!" came the exhausted plea. "Someone?"

A.J. went to the edge of the pit and leveled his gaze at the shivering girl. "Jeannie? Hang on, we got ya..."

Constructing a bosun's chair from the nylon rope he always carried on his bike, Liam and A.J. hauled Jeannie from the sinkhole, while Kris rode back to the Bluff and notified Sheriff Chavez and Deputy Halverson about their discovery. They crossed their fingers that Chavez would take the net gain of rescuing the missing girl and not prosecute them for trespassing in Old Town. Since their story of hearing Jeannie's call for help as they were riding past Old Town on the way to their fishing spot was somewhat if not entirely plausible, the gamble made sense—and to a large degree it worked. Turned loose with a warning and a reluctant thank you, the boys were transported back to town in Halverson's Bronco while Sheriff Chavez took Jeannie to the medical center in Gold Beach.

Halverson dropped the boys off at the diner, just before he was called away to a car fire on the Wedderburn Bridge section of Highway 101. All three friends were buzzing with adrenaline and excitement, and none of them knew how far from over the evening actually was.

80

The dinner rush on Fridays usually manifested in a packed dining room, with the single old-timers hunched over the bar, and families celebrating payday in the double line of booths opposite. Kris' mom ran the front-of-house, while his dad supervised the kitchen staff, one part head chef, one part orchestra conductor. But the only music audible was the crackle of a 45 RPM single courtesy of The Cars on the juke box, pulsing and retching like a sick cat from tinny ceiling speakers.

Since you're gone
I missed the peak sensation
Since you're gone
I took the big vacation

Since you're gone
Well, I never feel sedate
Since you're gone
Well, the moonlight ain't so great

Kris donned his cap and apron and went to work, while A.J. and Liam scooted into a booth. Burgers and Cokes came out automatically, and at the family discount—which often meant "free".

A.J. caught the milky eye of Kristof's grandmother behind the counter as she rolled out and filled a new batch of pirogies, offering a toast with his glass of Coke. She stared at him a moment and then returned to her work, leaving A.J. uncomfortable and a bit befuddled. He returned his attention to Liam and was about to mention possible origins for the glyph they'd seen, but the older boy was transfixed on something in the distance. A.J. turned to glance over his shoulder and saw the object of Liam's attention.

Molly leaned into the Asteroids machine and pounded away on the fire button, pulverizing wire-frame obstacles into space dust. A new arrival to Calico, she was 13 and just about to move into 8th grade in September. A pair of padded headphones encircled her neck, almost lost in the oversized hood of an orchid-colored pullover sweatshirt. The cord ran down her front to the Sony Walkman clipped to the waistband of her jeans. Her auburn hair was long on top, shaved on the back and sides, its length pulled back in a ponytail that displayed the buzzed under-portion and the multiple piercings in her ears. She was small and lithe, and shifted her weight back and forth on white leather Converse trainers.

When the two boys had finished their meals and bused their own plates to the wash tub behind the bar, Liam went to put a quarter on the Asteroids game in direct challenge to Molly, who had—in a short half hour— knocked his high score down to number two.

A.J. went into the back kitchen to confab with Kris and his grandmother. With Kris translating back and forth from English to Polish, A.J. showed a drawing of the strange glyph they'd seen at the Bluff and branded into Jeannie's wrist.

"Ask her if she's ever seen a symbol like this," A.J. instructed. Kris pointed at the drawing and asked his Grandmother, who simply peered at the two boys through her white eye and shook her head.

"*Nie*," was her soft reply.

A.J. was disappointed. The old lady was usually a font of Old World knowledge and trivia. She had at least a dozen ways of warding off the Evil Eye, and could predict the weather more accurately than the Farmer's Almanac.

Kris shrugged. "Sorry, dude." Then he blinked and remembered the 24-volume set of Time-Life Books he and his dad had found at a garage sale in Salem a few years ago. They were illustrated with all sorts of harrowing paintings of supernatural themes, which had scared Kris out of his wits when he was nine. "Oh, wait!" he blurted, snapping his fingers. "We have that set of *Man, Myth & Magic* back at the house!" He immediately regretted doing so, as it effectively blocked any hope of the guys hanging out at the diner for videogames and free cola. Now he'd be under pressure to leave work early and go wherever adventure led them.

Fortunately his mother, a Reubenesque woman with gray streaks in her pinned-up auburn hair, took note of the dining room—now largely vacant—and told Kris to hang up his apron for the night. A.J. made smalltalk with Mrs. Korolewski while his friend went to clean up, and got her permission for Kris to spend the night at his place for an epic *D&D* campaign they were supposedly finishing up.

Kris grabbed his jacket off a wall peg in the back, nodding toward the front door, where Liam and the "new girl" stood chatting. Molly looked decidedly unimpressed with Liam's tales of having built a set of nunchucks in shop class.

A.J. peered over his glasses as the four gathered by the door. "Who's this?" he asked.

Molly squinted at him. "*This* is Molly," she shot back.

"Her family bought the old Chambers place up on the hill," Liam explained. "They're real estate developers. Her brother was an all-state quarterback back in California."

A.J. flashed a look of disbelief at Liam. "Jesus, dude. What's her favorite color?"

"Purple," Molly smirked. "Your buddy here was saying you've been out at Old Town and found that missing girl, Jeannie?"

Kris flushed red and shoved his hands into the pockets of his jeans. "Yeah, that was us."

"Cool." Molly looked impressed for the first time since she'd entered the diner. "So what are you guys up to now?"

"We're going to look up a symbol we saw at the Bluff in my books and then we're going back out to Old Town," Kris blurted. "Wanna come?"

The idea of a girl tagging along on their expedition didn't sit well with A.J., though he wasn't sure why. Molly seemed okay, and Liam was sure doing his best to vouch for her while Kris blushed his way through the conversation. It was clear the two of them had no problem including her.

"Hold up," A.J. warned. "We haven't actually planned anything."

But before he knew what was happening, they were outside, heading around the back of the restaurant to the rustic home Kris shared with his parents and grandmother. Once in Kris' bedroom, with books spread out on the dingy rust-colored carpet, A.J. found his focus. He and Kris poured over the sections on angelic and alien symbols, while Molly looked at the volume on ESP and Liam rocked out to the mix tape in Molly's Walkman.

The music he heard was a revelation. A kid from rural Oregon with access to only a couple classic rock stations and a country station, Liam had been raised on a steady diet of bands referred to by single-word names: Zeppelin, Stones, Skynyrd, and bands that only had single words in their names to begin with: Styx, Rush, Kiss. Occasionally Mr. Korolewski would bring back a 45 from Portland for the diner's juke box. The Cars, Pretenders or Quarterflash. Something popular on that new MTV cable network—not that Calico had cable at all. But Molly's mix tape was a banquet of punk, post-punk and new romantic alternative rock that Liam could never have imagined existing. Siouxsie and the Banshees. Bauhaus. The Clash. Joy Division. Japan. This was high culture that kids from Los Angeles brought with them to the northern wilds as a gift to the natives. He was just hitting the opening drum cadence of Black Flag's "Gimme Gimme Gimme" when A.J. announced he'd found their mysterious icon in a section on alien languages.

Liam removed the thin pair of headphones, immediately realizing how loud he'd had the volume. "You found it?"

A.J. turned the book so the others could see it, producing his sketch of the symbol for comparison. "Doesn't say anything about what it means," he qualified, "just that it's been found at UFO crash sites and stuff." He was quite disappointed that its origin wasn't among the arcane scripts among the books. Surely that was more appropriate for Satanists.

Kris let out a low whistle and Molly chuckled nervously.

"Creeeeeepy," she said musically.

A.J. glanced at the alarm clock on Kris' nightstand. "Okay," he said, "it's almost 9. How's everyone for curfew?"

Liam grinned ear-to-ear. "Dude. *School's out!*"

Kris got the Alice Cooper reference and joined Liam singing incorrectly, "*...for the weekend!*"

Molly rolled her eyes in the way only a thirteen-year-old girl can do. "My folks are in Grant's Pass for a sales seminar. They left my brother in charge. *Technically.*"

"What does *technically* mean?" asked A.J.

"It means I can call him and say I'm spending the night at Alison's house, and he'll be fine with it."

A.J. thumbed through his mental Rolodex for any Alisons he might know. None sprang to mind. "Who's Alison?" he asked.

Molly shrugged, giving A.J. a half-smile that made him suddenly feel warm in his chest.

They took turns making calls to parents, the boys spinning the tale of the *D&D* game at A.J.'s—except for A.J., who said the game was at Liam's. Molly called her older brother, Bode, about spending the night at Alison's and being home before too late Saturday afternoon. That was just fine with Bode, who apparently had a girl over anyway.

And with the alibis set and the plan in place, A.J., Kris, Liam and Molly headed out on their bikes into the dark streets of Calico, Oregon.

∞

With battery-powered headlamps, they pedaled into the night, stopping first at Liam's garage, where the boys loaded their backpacks with miscellaneous gear: flashlights, road flares, a pair of Radio Shack walkie-talkies, and 100 feet of coiled nylon climbing rope, which Molly ended up slinging across her shoulder like a bandoleer. Liam also insisted on bringing a ten-foot length of one-inch PVC pipe in reference to the standard tool taken by all of his *D&D* characters on their adventures. It had started as a ten-foot length, but was now actually only 8-foot-four, as Liam's dad had cut as needed to fix the bathroom sink. Liam carried it under his arm like a jousting lance.

Molly had put her brother's latest mix tape into her Walkman, and had the volume set loud. Bode had the habit of naming his mixes after obscure literary references, and this one was called *I Sing the Body Electric*, after the Ray Bradbury short story. It consisted largely of guitar-based rock and new wave like Elvis Costello, The Vapors, and The Pretenders. As the Calico kids zoomed off toward Indian Bluff and beyond, Chrissy Hynde's vocal refrain swirled in Molly's ears:

Every day, every nighttime I feel

Mystery achievement you're so unreal

She felt almost as if Chrissy was speaking to her, on a primal, nostalgic, *Scooby Doo* level.

They cut off the access road as before, approaching Old Town from the southern curve. The moon sat obscured by a diffusion of high clouds, bathing the ruins of old Calico in a dim light. Rickety facades of the buildings lining Main Street poked up in silhouette, disappearing in the distance toward the mines.

They dropped their bikes in front of the saloon where they'd found Jeannie, deciding after some cajoling, daring and counter-daring to explore the hotel across the street. The structure was at this point no more than a hollow box, the wood of its construction rotten and creaking in the breeze. A.J. warned that it might collapse at any time, and was too dangerous to investigate at night, but Liam prevailed, citing the allegedly massive size of his testicles as his reason. Molly rolled her eyes, but volunteered to go with him anyway. The two of them disappeared inside, accompanied by Liam's PVC pipe.

Kris and A.J. decided that discretion—and not getting tetanus—was the better part of valor, and said they'd keep watch outside.

As Liam and Molly worked their way around the inside walls toward the old staircase, Liam used the plastic pole to tap and jab at various tears and ridges in the buckled floorboards. The hotel interior was dark and musty, filled with creaks and groans and the occasional jump scare when a rat crossed the beam of Molly's flashlight.

Aside from a century's worth of dust and holes in the floor where the boards had rotted and fallen in, the main level was devoid of anything interesting. The hotel had been one of the last structures to be abandoned when the town packed up to move, and had been thoroughly cleared out. Anything of value or historical significance had been looted by curious and adventuresome teens or souvenir hunters over the intervening years.

"Nothing much down here," Liam muttered.

Molly shone her flashlight across the lower half of the staircase to the second floor. "Stairs look okay."

Liam swallowed hard. "Um, yeah...sure."

A.J. peered in through one of the empty window frames. "Aww hell," he sighed. "They're gonna go upstairs." He turned back to Kris, who was frozen in a terrified tableau, eyes wide and fixed on the north end of Main Street.

At first Kris had thought it was the reflection of a car headlight, but as it moved, he began to pick out some detail. It was of a graceful, generally feminine shape, glowing a bright phosphorescent white at the center, and gradually diffusing to an invisible edge. It floated slowly, ethereally, from the corner of the old hardware store, on a diagonal path across Main Street to the collapsed warehouse on the opposite side.

It checked all of the boxes for being a ghost, and Kris stood petrified on the rotting hotel porch, knees locked in absolute fear.

A.J. stared at his friend in surprise. "Kris? Hey, what's up, buddy?"

Kris didn't answer, but A.J. could see beads of sweat beginning to form on his brow. Taking a cue from where his friend's eyes were focused, he quickly glanced the same direction, but saw nothing. The apparition had vanished.

"Did...did you see it?" Kris stammered.

"See what?"

"I...dunno. Looked like a..."

"Like a what?"

Kris began to unlock his muscles as the sense of threat faded and his fight-or-flight response subsided in kind. "Nothing," he said quietly.

Inside the hotel, Molly led Liam up the age-worn staircase, still standing due to its oak construction alone. Nonetheless, eight steps from the top landing, Molly put her foot in precisely the wrong spot, and punched a hole in a stair tread.

She fell forward with a grunt. "Ugh. Shit."

"You okay?" Liam was immediately two stairs above, turning back to offer her assistance. "Here, grab my pole," he smirked.

Molly again rolled her eyes. "Jesus," she sighed. "How long have you been waiting to make that joke?"

She took hold of the PVC pipe regardless, and Liam anchored them as she removed her leg from the sundered stair and hopped lightly up to the top landing.

"Long enough, apparently," Liam grinned.

The hotel had eight guest rooms on the second floor, four on each side of the gallery. Unfortunately the floor itself had caved in over the western corner of the structure, leaving that wing inaccessible. Molly and Liam were restricted to the eastern wing, in whose hallway they stood on creaky floorboards.

Taking great care with every step, the two tiptoed to the farthest room, noticing its door had come off the top hinge, and was sitting open at a cocked angle. Molly, being small and fearless, squeezed past the crooked door and flashed her light around the room. A century-old wrought iron bed frame rusted in the corner, next to a pile of wood and glass debris that had probably been a nightstand and oil lamp at some point. The space was otherwise empty.

Molly ducked back into the gallery hall. "Nothing," she said, directing her light toward the second room, which was minus a door altogether.

They entered the second room, flashlights revealing a space almost identical to the first, but without the bed frame and debris. Liam could tell Molly was getting antsy, but didn't want to be the first to chicken out.

"There's nothing here," she said. "I'm gonna check the third room."

Then she was gone, and Liam stood alone in a dusty room, in a creaky hotel, in an Oregon ghost town. A shiver ran down his spine and he turned to follow, but stopped when the beam from his flashlight hit something shiny on the floor by the doorway. He leaned the plastic pole against the corner of the room and bent down, brushing some dust and wear from a large coin, turning it over in his hand.

It was silver, with an eagle on one side, and a seated woman holding a shield that said LIBERTY on the other. The date stamp was 1870.

Excited beyond words, Liam pocketed the coin and grabbed his PVC pole from the corner. He stepped back out into the hall as Molly put her foot through a rotten floorboard and fell forward again.

"Ugh. Goddamn it!" she huffed.

Again, Liam was at her side, offering assistance.

"Here, take—"

"Yeah, yeah, give me your pole."

Liam braced himself and hauled Molly from the hole in the floor. She was not amused.

"You've never dated, have you?" she inquired.

"Sure I have. Lots of times," he said. As he spoke, Liam's cheek twitched, signaling Molly that he was lying.

"Uh huh," Molly sighed, rolling her eyes at an Olympic level of proficiency. "Let's check the last room and get out of here."

As they turned toward the last guest room, door missing like the second, a hissed shout echoed from downstairs.

"Hey! Guys! Get down here!"

Liam and Molly made eye contact for a moment, and without saying a word, headed for the stairs.

They exited the hotel onto the sagging porch, Liam thrilled to share the news of his find.

"Hey, guess what I found upstairs..."

Molly cut him off with a slap to the arm, nodding at A.J. and Kris, who were frozen in place, eyes locked on the north end of town. Multiple apparitions floated from a vanishing point in the distance, dispersing into town among the rotting structures and ruins of Old Calico.

A.J. pointed. "Is that what you saw before?"

Kris nodded in the affirmative. "Just one, though."

Liam had questions. "Wait. Before? When did you...what are...Jesus, look how many!"

"I count about a dozen," Molly said, switching off her flashlight and stepping silently from the hotel porch.

"Wait, Molly!" A.J. hissed. "Where are you going?"

"I wanna get closer," was the whispered reply, then she disappeared into the shadows of the ruins along Main Street.

A.J. awoke from his reverie, whether out of a sense of obligation to protect the new girl from whatever was flitting from the mines, or a sense of self-preservation lest anything happen to Molly that would be awkward to explain to parents and authorities. "Come on," he instructed. "Try to keep to the shadows." Then he was off as well.

Liam and Kris followed, not to be outdone by a "chick and a nerd", taking off in a stooped run straight from a bad WWII movie. Liam muttered, "Serpentine," as he zigged and zagged toward the livery stable.

Molly peered around the corner of the stable and felt a cold hand on the back of her neck. Spinning instantly, her left arm shot out and knocked A.J.'s flashlight to the ground. "Sheeeit!" she hissed through clenched teeth. "Don't do that!"

"Sorry," A.J. protested. "I couldn't see where you'd stopped." He tried to look past her toward Main Street, but the silhouette of her head blocked his view. Her hair smelled like strawberry Suave.

A sudden burst of light erupted from the night sky, like a photographer's strobe. All four of the teens cast their eyes skyward, as if to check the weather for an impending storm, but it was the same moon slung high behind the same scattered clouds. What had changed?

Molly was first to notice. "Hey," she whispered, gesturing down Main Street toward the mine entrance in the distance. "They're gone."

The boys stepped gingerly away from the corner of the stable and verified that, yes, the apparitions, which had populated the old ghost town just moments ago, had vanished. The ruins of Old Town sat as still and silent as ever.

"What now?" A.J. asked, clearly shaken by the sudden, eerie quiet.

Liam flicked on his flashlight and stepped into the dusty street. "I'm gonna check out the mine." He knew only the bravest of older high school kids ever ventured anywhere near the mine opening. If the rest of Old Town was hazardous due to the sinkholes and century-old buildings which threatened to collapse at any moment, the mine was exponentially so. No excuse was good enough to spin at Sheriff Chavez that would avoid the most epic grounding by his parents if anything happened in there. Liam was therefore certain it would impress Molly. He took a deep breath and prepared his legs to carry him to the end of Main Street and up the incline to the mouth of the tunnel. A.J. made a frustrated motion to make him stop. Molly rolled her eyes so hard it gave her a headache.

"HOLY SHIT!"

Everyone jumped, turning toward Kris, who stood frozen to the ground, absolutely petrified, gaping at something at the far end of his flashlight beam. Something on the other side of the livery window. As the others crowded around their friend to take in his view, their mouths each fell open in amazement.

A slender, pale face, long-haired and sunken-eyed, stared back at them. Although lean, the jaw was square, the brow furrowed in a look of rudderless shock. Instantly, the boys knew exactly who it was.

Eric Somerville.

He was alive—or at least appeared so—albeit slightly the worse for wear. But he was solid and real, unlike the apparitions they'd seen previously. A.J. scrambled to the stable door, which had been reduced to a barricade of cracked and moldy planks that leaned criss-crossed against the sides of the opening. The roof had mostly fallen in over time, and the structure was unstable enough that nobody wanted to leave Eric stuck inside.

The others followed A.J., pitching in to remove enough of the broken planks to create an opening wide enough for him to get through.

Pushing his glasses high onto his nose and aiming his flashlight into the dark interior, A.J. stepped into the old livery stable. Broken crates and a few rusted barrel hoops were the only contents, save Eric himself. The boy was a strapping six-footer, with shoulder-length chestnut hair. He was clad in well-worn blue jeans, his feet and upper torso bare. Turning in the beam of the flashlight, his mouth opened and he tried to speak, but no sound emerged.

A.J. approached cautiously. "Eric?" he croaked. "Hey, man..." As he slowly padded toward the boy, he happened to glance down, and noticed the same strange glyph that they'd all seen up at Indian Bluff, burned into the dirt floor. A.J. made a point to side-step around it.

As A.J. came toward Eric, he could see the older kid blink, and suddenly turn to look at him.

"Hello?" came the hoarse whisper. "Are you real?"

A.J. suddenly felt his fear turn to sympathy, and his heart sank. "Yeah, man. We got ya. Come with me." He took Eric's arm, looking down to see that the same glyph Jeannie was found branded with—the same glyph that they were finding all over the ground in Old Town and at the Bluff—was likewise branded into his palm.

As A.J. slowly guided Eric toward the livery door, carefully keeping away from the shape seared into the dirt, he tried a basic line of questioning. "Do you remember what happened to you?"

Eric's eyes were blank. "No. Where's Jeannie?"

"She's okay, man. We found her."

"She's okay?"

"Yeah, buddy. She's fine."

"I-I need to get home."

A.J. guided Eric by the arm out to the remaining three. Eric was walking tender-footed on the stony ground. Liam shrugged out of his baggy Army jacket and offered it to Eric, whom it fit much better. Together and in complete silence, the four walked Eric back to the edge of Old Town where their bikes awaited. The question was really how to get him home, as they were one bike short. After a bit of petty logistical debate, Molly volunteered to ride on the rear rack of the Kricycle and let Eric use her purple unisex BMX.

They rode back in silence, surrounding Eric to make sure he didn't veer randomly off-course.

When the headlights hit them, A.J. was convinced it was another brilliant flash signifying one of them was about to disappear. One by one, each kid skidded to a halt at the outside of the curve, shielding their eyes from the glare of halogen headlamps. A black 1980 Ford Fairmont sedan sat idling in the middle of the road, between them and Perry's Bridge, a structure straddling one of the many tributaries of the Rogue River. The first of the old timber access paths stretched off the main road just a few dozen yards beyond, but they'd have to cross the bridge to get there.

Kris was already sweating from the ride, but his exertion had become panic. "Who is that?"

A.J. had heard stories about government agents in black cars showing up during UFO investigations, threatening individuals, or making them "disappear". He had no desire for such an encounter. "No one we want to meet," was his answer.

"They're blocking the bridge," Liam observed.

"Really?" Molly sighed. "Hadn't noticed."

The black car revved its engine from a hundred yards away, tires screaming on the old asphalt road. With a steep, wooded hillside to the right, the river to the left, and a menacing vehicle blocking their access to the back road into town, there was only one option.

"Follow me!" A.J. shouted, spinning his bike on its rear tire and pedaling hard the way they'd just come. The others followed suit, trying to keep up—Kris pumping his legs furiously with the extra body to carry.

The car roared up the road, painting their backs in white light, pulling closer with each second.

They rounded the turn and were hitting the crest of a rise near a turnout when A.J. suddenly pulled off the road and stood in the saddle, walking on his bike pedals as he nosed up the hillside, thick with trees. Eric followed, then Liam. Kris' bike struggled under the awkwardness of two riders, and he skidded, almost ditching the bike along with Molly. Gripping one wrist with her other hand, arms encircling his waist, she held on for dear life, sneakered feet sticking to the pegs on the rear wheel. He recovered with a subtle adjustment to the front fork, and followed the others in doubling back.

The Ford flew past them, losing track of the riders in the woods. It skidded into a 180-

degree turn, fishtailing as the engine revved again.

Without wasting a moment, A.J. steered down the hillside and onto the road in their original direction. All too quickly, the black Ford was close behind them again, engine snarling as they flew toward the bridge.

This would be dicey.

If the car so much as clipped one of them, there was nothing to stop them from wiping out on the rocks and freezing water. There was no way to avoid the vehicle on a small timber bridge that was only one car wide to begin with. A collective surge of adrenaline hit the group and bike pedals churned faster. They hit the bridge at top speed, knowing there was only one way to go: forward.

Knobby tires vibrated across timber beams, and the car was on them, its front bumper almost knocking the Kricycle. Molly turned momentarily behind to look and was blinded by the headlights. Burying her face in Kris' sweaty back might have been a questionable thought mere minutes ago, but now it was the only semblance of safety in a moment of potential oblivion.

The Ford's engine roared.

Then they were across to the far side, and A.J. led them up onto the timber access trail. The car squealed its tires and tried to turn, then recovered and gunned its engine up toward the access. With brights still glaring, it nosed its grill into the woods, probing the trail slowly. The large sedan was not as agile on the soft, uneven ground. The bikes were much faster and more maneuverable in this environment. A.J. and Eric broke off down a trail to the left. Liam, Kris and Molly to the right. Within a few minutes, the sound of the Ford's engine grew distant as the car ceased pursuit and backed out of the timber access road.

Before long, the kids had reunited on the outskirts of town. When they got within sight of the Sommerville house, A.J. had a sudden thought.

"Hey, Eric, when you tell your folks about us finding you, maybe don't mention Old Town, huh? We weren't exactly supposed to be out there."

Eric braked to a halt and dismounted the borrowed bicycle, offering it back to Molly. "Sure, man," Eric acknowledged, more lucid than A.J. had seen him that night. Maybe the hard ride while being chased by the mystery car had put his brain back on track. "You found me in a ditch off the main road. That's all I remember."

As Molly accepted her bike back and swung her leg across the frame, Eric winked at her. Ordinarily she might have found it unwarranted and creepy, but in this instance, it was more like a secret code between people who had endured a crisis together.

"Chavez would give you guys hell," he said blankly, although A.J. could have sworn the corner of his right lip curled up almost enough to be considered a smirk. Then any indication of levity vanished as he added, "Not to mention whoever was in that black Ford."

"Thanks, man," A.J. said, and the others echoed in kind. "Too bad we didn't have your Nova."

Liam nodded in agreement. "Yeah, that machine would've blown the doors off that Fairmont."

Eric allowed himself a quiet chuckle. "Damn straight."

As the four friends aimed their bikes back into Calico, Eric waved awkwardly. "Thank *you*," he said solemnly, and turned toward the porch light of his parents' home.

"What's the plan?" Molly asked after several moments. "My brother thinks I'm at Allison's tonight."

"We still don't know what's up with those glyphs," A.J. Said.

Kris yawned. "And we're not gonna figure it out tonight."

"Anyone up for some *D&D*?" Liam suggested. "I can run my *Death Island* scenario."

"I hate that scenario," Kris complained. "It's always a T-P-K."

Molly frowned. "What's 'T-P-K'?"

"Total Party Kill," A.J. explained, not surprised that her response was a simple shrug. "Anyway, I'm tired."

They turned off North Bank Rogue River Road onto 1st Avenue, flying past the Calico Saloon, 1st Ave Grill, and the auto shop. Traffic was almost nonexistent, and they wove and swooped down toward Cedar Street, lost in their own individual thoughts. A.J. had pretty much called it, and the others would follow suit. Their adventure was over, at least for now. There would be more research, and probably another expedition back into Old Town, and possibly into the mine. But there would be more preparation, more due diligence. And they had to make sure Sheriff Chavez didn't investigate Eric's return in too much detail.

They slowed to a stop as they passed Cedar, and 1st Avenue began to climb toward Union Street. Pulling to a stop at the corner by the T-shirt shop, just a block south of the diner, they slapped hands and exchanged smiles at a job well done.

"So our overnight plans fell through," A.J. said. "That's all we need to tell our folks."

Liam saluted. "Tomorrow, then?"

"Meet you at the diner," A.J. promised.

They pedaled off in their separate ways, A.J. backtracking up 1st Avenue toward home. He stood in the saddle as he pumped up the incline of Lamont Street, breathing hard, heart pounding in his chest.

It had been quite a day.

Cruising across 4th Avenue, he hit Hillcrest at blinding speed, flashing back on the day's events, and the music that had pulled him out of bed in the first place.

Burn out the day

Burn out the night

I'm not the one to tell you what's wrong or what's right

I've seen suns that were freezing and lives that were through

Well I'm burning, I'm burning, I'm burning for you

ℬ

Saturday morning arrived in a salmon-pink sky and puffy clouds, and the four friends gathered at the Silver City Diner for a quick breakfast before deciding on their itinerary. Unfortunately their plans were waylaid by one Sheriff Chavez, who insisted on grilling the four kids about their whereabouts the previous night. Apparently Eric followed through, as Chavez was satisfied that their story matched his. The kids had been heading upriver for a camp-out and had run across an unconscious Eric in a ditch by the road. They'd been nowhere near Old Town. Fair enough.

At least both of the missing teens had been found, and Chavez was hesitant to push too hard for punishment when the end result had been a public service. In fact, there was a bit of PR still to be done. An interview for the local paper, and a nice reward, which Molly declined to partake in, since she already received a healthy weekly allowance. The boys insisted, however. If nothing else, a thousand dollars was easier to split evenly four ways.

By the time they'd met their civil commitments, there was no time left to head out for further study of the alien glyphs. Sunday was marred by a downpour, and the final week of classes further curtailed their adventures.

School finally let out for the summer on Wednesday, and Thursday morning found all four pedaling their bikes out to Indian Bluff, bright and early. The shape which less than a week ago had been seared into the asphalt of the turnout was gone, as if it had never existed.

A quick recon into Old Town verified a distinct lack of glyphs there as well.

A.J. decided to track down Eric at his parents' home, and was dismayed to learn the young man had followed through on his promise to leave town right after graduation.

Mr. Wells had been offered a new, better-paying job in Salem, and Jeannie had gone with her father, probably happy for the change in environment, even if she couldn't be with Eric.

It was decided among the four friends that the Mystery at Old Town would remain their secret lore—told only to the most trusted people. How they'd found alien teleportation glyphs in the ground, and had rescued the missing teenagers, outsmarting the local Sheriff, and outrunning the mysterious black Ford, just before the end of the school year.

With pockets full of reward money, they planned a summer full of adventure, from *D&D* at A.J.'s house, to day trips into Gold Beach to check out the summer movies. A new Steven Spielberg flick about an alien lost on Earth and the kids who befriend it had just come out.

This would be good.

෨

Written in 2019 as a nostalgic nod to the "kids on bikes" sub-genre of scifi/horror (exemplified by *E.T.*, *The Goonies*, and more recently, *Stranger Things*).

The town of Calico, Oregon is a wholesale invention, so don't try to find it. Although the characters and events are likewise fictional, everything is couched in familiar experiences I had—and people I knew—growing up in the sleepy seaside community of Aptos, California in from the mid-1970s to the mid-1980s.

ABOUT THE AUTHOR

Todd Downing's love affair with genre storytelling dates back to his consumption of classic radio dramas and comic books as a child in the 1970s, which broadened into a general appreciation for scifi and fantasy media of all kinds.

He grew up in the greater San Francisco Bay Area, writing and drawing from a young age, his works ever-present in 'zines, school literary journals and local newspapers, and eventually on film. He married his high school sweetheart and moved to Seattle in 1991 where he began to write professionally, and worked as an artist in the videogame industry until his publishing company became a full time operation, while raising two children amid the chaos.

Downing is the primary author and designer of over fifty roleplaying titles, including *Arrowflight, RADZ, Airship Daedalus*, and the official *Red Dwarf* RPG. He continues to write genre fiction for stage, film, comics, audio, and adventure gaming products.

Widowed to cancer in 2005, Downing remarried in 2009 and currently enjoys an empty nest in Port Orchard, Washington, with his wife, a rescued huskador, and a flock of unruly chickens.

Join the author's mailing list:
www.todddowning.com

Thrilling pulp adventure!
www.airshipdaedalus.com

Read the adventures of the
Airship *Daedalus:*
A Shield Against the Darkness
(Book #1)
Assassins of the Lost Kingdom
(Book #2, by E.J. Blaine)
The Golden City
(Book #3)
Legend of the Savage Isle
(Book #4)

Plus:

AEGIS Tales
A retro-pulp anthology, volume 1

AVAILABLE NOW
in ebook and print!